CRY
OF THE
CROW

LAURA BARRINGTON

PAGE PUBLISHING, INC.
New York, NY

First originally published by Page Publishing, Inc. 2019

ISBN 978-1-64462-955-0 (Paperback)
ISBN 978-1-64462-956-7 (Digital)

Printed in the United States of America

In loving memory of my son Chase

CHAPTER 1

The streetlamp over the parking lot hummed and cast a dim yellow light which reflected in the puddles of water that lay in the potholes of the alley. She could hear the rain splashing from the tires of the cars as they passed by on the street a hundred feet ahead of her. The raindrops splatting against her face didn't seem to distract her as she leaned against the back of the building in the shadows cast from the row of historic buildings and puffed at the cigarette she held between her fingers. She drew on the cigarette with long intentional drags and watched the ember on the end grow longer before pitching it to the ground and snuffing it out with the toe of her shoe. She turned suddenly toward a movement which caught her eye, and she watched as a cat skulked along the edge of the building, trying to avoid the droplets of rain falling over everything. It behaved skittishly and jumped at every sound coming from the city as it looked around for the source of the noise before proceeding on its path.

"You don't like the rain, little kitty?" she asked the cat as it continued its walk close to the wall of the building protected by the overhang of the roof. "I find it refreshing as it washes away all the filth of the world. When the sun comes out the next morning, everything looks fresh and new."

Stepping out of the shadows, she walked slowly, but with intent, alone down the alley as she listened to the sounds of the rain around her as it hit the roofs of the buildings, cars, and plastic trash bags and barrels lining the alleyway for pickup. She could hear the buzzing sound of the security lights, the occasional screech of tires, and her own shoes splashing through the raised water. Unhampered by the rain and occasional flash of lightning followed by the rumble of thunder, she continued her trek toward her destination as she had come to finish something. In fact, she thought to herself, *The weather is quite fitting for a cleansing.*

Her timing was impeccable as she watched the man exit the rear entrance of the office building and hurriedly climb into his car. With a determined posture and air of confidence about her, she approached the man sitting in his red Jaguar in the parking lot behind the prosecutor's office. She walked casually to the driver's door and tapped lightly on the window. She had been anticipating this moment, and she felt the blood begin to pulse through her veins as she bent down toward the driver who had engaged the auto window opener. The beating of her heart was deafening in her ears, and her hands shook a little as she placed a cigarette between her lips and asked if he had a light. The man fumbled in his suit jacket and retrieved a lighter, flicking it before bringing the flame closer to her. Taking his hands in hers, she bent closer to the flame and drew the cigarette until the end burned bright orange. She could see he was clearly unsettled by her gesture but excited by it as she gazed intently in his eyes.

"It's extremely wet out here tonight. Can I give you a lift somewhere?" he asked as his eyes left hers and gazed the span of her body. He continued to stare at her exposed breasts from the gap in the leather jacket she wore that fit her like a glove, as well as the leather pants which gave her outfit the appearance of being one continuous piece of material tailored to her perfect shape.

"I was hoping you would ask." She smiled and pitched the cigarette to the side as she strode to the other side of the car and climbed in, making herself comfortable in the passenger seat. She could still smell the newness of the leather covering the interior of the car, but it was overrun by the scent of his greasy, sweaty, overweight body mixed with the stench of his cologne, which wreaked too much spice. She turned to him with a smile that covered her face but was void in her eyes. In fact, her eyes reflected the absence of human emotion but went unnoticed by him.

"Where might I have the pleasure of dropping you?" He smiled at her with a half-cocked grin, which told her what he had in mind. Her stomach rolled at the mere thought of his fat stubby fingers even touching her flesh, but she had to fight back the urge to vomit so that she could be convincing.

"I suppose that depends on your plans." She smiled in response while running the end of her fingers along the top of his right hand that sat atop the gear shift of the car. Inside, her stomach churned as it had not yet settled. She felt she would be sick any minute, but she kept herself calm and leaned toward him.

He nearly lost control of the steering wheel before regaining his composure and explaining he had just the place in mind.

The stranger was already aware of their destination as she had been following the prosecutor for several weeks now. She nearly laughed aloud as he turned on the signal and turned right into the hotel parking lot where he asked her to remain waiting until she saw him place a stop in the door.

"No problem," the stranger agreed, sitting back in the seat, watching as he entered the door to the hotel. "You are quite predictable, Mr. Prosecutor. Luck be with me tonight, but I can't say the same for you. It's time to turn the tables and return to you what you gave. I hope you find it to your liking, but something tells me you won't."

CHAPTER 2

Detective Hough awoke with a start from the repeated sound of a buzzing noise he heard coming from his nightstand next to the bed. He could tell from the flashing light accompanying the sound it was his cell phone. He gently pulled his arm from under his son's head so as not to awaken him as he fumbled to locate the source of his annoyance. He had, once again, allowed himself to fall asleep while reading to Gabriel before putting his son to sleep in his own bed.

"Hough here." He groaned groggily into the phone, wiping his eyes while he tried gathering his thoughts. "I'll be right there." He assured the caller before placing the phone back on the nightstand and turning to gaze down at his sleeping son. He couldn't help but smile at the angelic face of his sleeping son as he pulled the blanket farther up over him and tossed his hair softly. David exited the room quietly and walked down the hall and tapped lightly on another door.

"Ms. Mary, it's me, David," he whispered through the door. "I am sorry to disturb you at this hour, but I have to go out. I just received a call."

"I am coming." He could hear her reply as she walked softly across the floor and turned the knob to her bedroom door. His apologetic face was greeted with a smile and a pat to each cheek of his face. "I will start some coffee for you."

"I am going to need it." He smiled back before turning to head back down the hallway toward the shower. His mind strayed to thoughts of how he could ever explain to Ms. Mary how important she had become to him and Gabriel. He wasn't sure if mere words could ever describe how thankful he was for her having been placed in their lives when he needed a strong but gentle soul to help guide him back to life. In fact, to him she had become a godsend. She was a widower after thirty-seven years of marriage. She and her husband had been unable to conceive a child of their own, so through the years, while her husband worked, Mary would spend time with the ladies in the community, and if any of their children needed tending to, she would offer her time. It was easy for her to see how many of the mothers rarely had time to even tend to their own needs, so she would spend hours at one of their homes so the mother could relax and, even at times, simply take a nap. Mary had shown each of the children her love and, in return, was loved by many. She would often receive cards and phone calls from them, checking to see how she was and if there was anything they could do for her. She didn't hesitate for even a moment to come to his aid when his wife was killed in an accident, leaving him to care for their four-month-old son alone at that time. Miss Mary had allowed him to grieve without judgment and had an uncanny ability to bring a grieving soul back to the living by helping them recognize the other things in life that are important.

David poured a cup of coffee before filling his thermos with the remainder and making his way to the garage where he climbed in his Jeep. He situated his thermos in the passenger seat and placed his mug in the console holder, and releasing the garage door, he exited the garage and drove the graveled drive to the end before turning onto the paved road leading into town. It was still dark as the sun hadn't yet risen, and his headlights glowed against the light fog which lingered close to the ground. It was nights like these in this area which made driving more difficult as one's headlights barely made a dent in the complete darkness of the forest and the fog made them appear even dimmer. He doubted he had too many worries with animals moving around at this hour, but they are animals and can be unpredictable, so he let up on the gas pedal and lowered his speed by ten miles per hour.

David enjoyed the peace and quiet that living out of town afforded him, but he often questioned if he was providing Gabriel enough socialization with his peers but quickly dismissed the thought as Ms. Mary would ensure he received what he needed in his absence.

He enjoyed the sounds of the nature he was surrounded by, but he noticed on some nights that he lay awake, unable to sleep, the silence surrounding him was nearly deafening. He would walk outside on his deck some nights, and even with a clear sky full of brilliant stars, he was unable to see his hand just a few inches from his face. He could identify different species by the sounds they made before they ever made their appearance out of curiosity.

David and his father worked on the designs to their home based on ideas from his wife and plans he liked as well. The property had been in her family for generations, so she knew the topography and was able to help them find the perfect location for their home, meeting all their criteria. The front had to look out over the lake, so his wife could drink her coffee on the front porch and stare out at the stillness of the lake of the morning. They both enjoyed nature, and it was still only fifteen minutes to the quiet town of Clare, Michigan. It was a small town but considered a fairly adequately sized place compared to other small towns. There's a familiarity between the locals with a family oriented feel to it, but big enough to not know everyone.

David could see the glow of the town getting brighter the closer he got to the city. He was only a few minutes out from the outskirts of the town, so he picked up his speed again. Arriving at his destination, he pulled through the barriers and made his way toward the location of the hotel where he could see his fellow officers on the scene clearly shaken and in horror by what they witnessed inside room 127. He could see a crowd already gathering on the sides of the police tape, which indicated a barrier they weren't permitted to pass beyond. He continued making his way into the building and advised he wanted them to extend the barrier and to not allow anyone in unless they were approved by him first.

David pushed the door open to the room, and what his eyes beheld before him was a sight he had never seen in his entire career as an officer of the law. Never had he ever imagined in his career or such an occurrence to take place in this sleepy little town. His eyes never beheld such a gruesome murder as what he saw at this moment—a completely impaled prosecuting attorney who had clearly been tortured before meeting his tragic demise, evident by his tongue which had been pulled as far as it would go and spliced down the center and secured in its position by a piece of metal placed against his upper and lower teeth. His eyelids had been stapled open so he would have to watch, as his killer carved the symbols he witnessed on the body into the flesh of his forearms, which now dangled void of movement toward the floor with drying streams of blood that trickled down his fingers and dripped into small puddles on the floor.

"You might want to take a look at this," an officer suggested, waving his hand for David to follow him.

Written on the stand in the victim's blood below a drawing of a crow in Irish, "Ta an Morrigan tar ar ais" was neatly scribed. David quickly pulled his phone from his pocket and googled the words and the crow. With a perplexed expression and furrow of his brow, he tried to make a connection which made sense. Counselor McCain was clearly Irish, but what does the goddess Morrigan have to do with the manner in which he had been executed? David asked himself before looking around the room for more clues that might help him to understand what happened here a few hours earlier.

"Who first found the crime scene?" David inquired from one of the officers.

"I believe it was Sergeant Jones and Officer Murphy, sir," the officer replied, pointing in the direction of the two uniformed men, who were clearly distraught over their discovery. The desk clerk seated close by was even more upset and traumatized than the officers as she covered her face with her hands, unable to take in any more of the horrific scene than she had earlier.

David made his way to where the officers and desk clerk were and asked if there were anything he could get them at the moment. They all shook their heads no and appeared anxious to provide the details of their find so they could be excused to leave.

"Can you begin by telling me why you were here to even make the discovery?" he began his inquiry.

"We received a call at the station from his wife who said she had talked to him just as he was leaving the office and would be straight home," Jones began. "She said she waited a couple of hours, thinking maybe he stopped off at the pub with friends, but when she tried to call and he didn't answer his phone, she became worried. Murphy and I were in the area and located his car, so we stopped in at the desk to check if he had reserved a room, and this lady provided us the room number. We walked down the corridor and knocked on the door several times before pushing it open since it was already ajar. You can imagine our shock, and we called it in immediately, sir."

"Why would you check at the hotel first?" Hough asked the officers, looking for understanding.

"Well, sir, it isn't news to anyone that the prosecutor enjoyed the company of hired women," one of the officers began, looking at the other for backup. "We arrest them, and he gets them right back out. He is often seen in their company and states he is trying to be of assistance to the ladies in turning their lives around and giving them a chance. This is one of the places he brings them, so we thought our chances of finding him here were good."

"Thank you, gentlemen, for your time," David assured them both. "If you have nothing further, I will speak with the hotel staff now."

"No, sir, that is all we know." They both agreed and wasted no time leaving once excused.

David turned to the clerk and made the few steps back to where she sat and placed his hand on one of her shoulders before proceeding.

"I know this is difficult for you to talk about, ma'am, but did you see anyone with Mr. McCain when he checked in?" David asked as he turned to her direction.

"He was alone when he reserved the room," she replied, unable to remove her hands from her face. "He said he had a couple of drinks at the bar and didn't think he should risk driving home for the night."

"So he didn't mention having company or that he was expecting anyone?" David continued.

"No," she responded. "In fact, he used the interior corridor to his room. If he left, he used the door to the parking lot of each corridor."

"Does the hotel keep video surveillance of the premises?" David asked.

"Yes, we do, but it doesn't cover the entire parking lot. It mainly covers the corridors and entry doors," she informed him.

"I need you to show me the video," David urged, encouraging the manager to take him to the office so they could view the tape.

The desk clerk stood and continued to try to shield her view away from the body by cupping her hands around her eyes so she could only see what was directly in front of her. David rewound the video to the time she thought Mr. McCain had arrived and was able to see him talking with her at the front desk, and clearly he did use the interior corridor to his room. They fast-forwarded to him entering the room and coming back out a few minutes later and walking to the doorway at the end of the hall to the parking lot. Instead of leaving the building, he appeared to have placed something in the door to prop it open before returning back to his room. It was difficult to see his room door from the angle of the camera to see if it had been closed completely behind him. Several minutes passed before David saw what appeared to be a female opening the door to the hall and retrieving the paper apparently placed there by the counselor. He was unable to get a clear view of her. It seemed she was trying to avoid having her face seen. They watched as she approached the door to the counselor's room and entered. They fast-forwarded the video, but it appeared to end and hadn't shown anyone leaving or anyone else entering before the arrival of the officers.

"Why does the video stop there?" David asked, unable to understand why the recording stopped.

"The company only provides surveillance during certain hours. If nothing occurs, they clear the video and start again," she explained.

David turned, excusing himself before making his way out of the office and practically running back to the scene of the crime. He carefully made his way into the room and was cautious not to interfere with the crime scene. David checked the window to discover it was still locked. His eyes spanned the room, and he even checked the bathroom and the door conjoining with the next, but it was locked. David couldn't figure out how she could possibly have gotten out without the camera picking her up unless she spent hours in the room. He questioned his certainty it was actually even a woman he had seen before asking himself if the person knew when the surveillance would end.

Making his way out of the hotel toward his car for the drive to the office, David could see the press had arrived. That was one thing you could be sure of in a town this size: news travels fast. Pushing his way through the cameras, he declined to make any comments as the family had not yet been notified. In today's society with technology everywhere, people had no problem posting everything their phones could record with no consideration for the families or victims. Most of the time, the videos only show what the person filming wants to show, so the viewer never gets the entire scenario. The most unsettling part to David was the mass amount of people who are so willing to believe what they see without having complete knowledge of the event.

"I am going to need those videos for evidence," David advised one of the officers on the scene as he made his way to his car. "Make sure I have a copy on my desk as soon as they can be duplicated."

Now came the most difficult part of his job—notifying the family, David thought to himself as he climbed in his Jeep and made the short drive to the newly widowed wife's home. Although the shock that comes with losing a loved one, especially from violent means, can also be the best time to gather information which might be pertinent to solving the crime. He still felt a long sense of forlorn for those left behind to deal with the tragic and unexpected loss of their loved one. There were many things about his job he loved, but this was definitely not one of them. David pulled into the driveway of their expansive home and climbed from the Jeep with heavy shoulders. He walked slowly up the sidewalk to the large entry door, and locating the door bell, he gave it a push and waited quietly for a response.

CHAPTER 3

The stranger stood at the back of the crowd that had gathered outside the hotel in the parking lot, watching the detective as he climbed in his Jeep and drove off. "I wish I could be there as he tells your family how your rotten ass died," she whispered so the other onlookers couldn't hear her. "Only now will they know even slightly how I felt when you stole my life from me. There's no way your family couldn't have known how you provided such a lavish lifestyle for them on your wages, as well as the community turning their blind eyes."

She watched until she saw them load the body into the emergency squad for transport to the morgue before turning to make her way across the parking lot and down a path along the wooded lot next to the hotel, disappearing into the trees and brush. Making her way down the windy path, she could smell the river ahead and held her pace.

"They should have listened to my father," she said aloud as she took a seat next to the riverbank. "He was an honorable man, and they tainted his reputation with their lies. It is time for me to make sure that everyone knows the truth and these evil bastards are stopped. They have no idea how much their lives are all about to change. This town will see a cleansing like they never knew. You are all about to fall from your high horses and reap what you have sown."

She picked up a rock and sailed it across the water, watching each ripple with every skip it made become larger and larger until it joined the others and disappeared.

"Such is life," the stranger spoke out loud. "One small ripple can change the flow of everything. I plan to make a big splash here so the ripples have a lasting effect for time to come. I won't allow them to ever forget what they allowed to happen."

She remained squatting by the water's edge for sometime, listening to the birds squawk in the trees nearby at her disturbance of their space and watched the water move slowly downstream, captivating her thoughts for a moment. She shook her head side to side as though she were shaking out the voices that seemed to be screaming over her, and she quickly stood and nearly ran up the narrow path along the river's edge.

CHAPTER 4

"Hi. Detective Hough?" David heard a soft voice say, more like a question than certainty. He turned to look over his shoulder as he sat at the counter sipping at his cup of steaming black coffee and running through his mind the pictures he had visually taken while trying to recall any recent cases of anyone who would have reason to want to not just kill a man but also sadistically torture him in what appears to be a ritualistic offering.

"Yes, I am Detective Hough," he replied, smiling. "Is there something I can help you with?"

"I certainly hope so," she replied with a bright smile lighting across her face.

"Have we met somewhere before?" David inquired, knowing he would have remembered her. "You don't look familiar, ma'am."

"We haven't had an opportunity to meet yet," she continued. "My name is Aislinn, and I am an investigative reporter and new here in town. I was hoping you had a few minutes you could spare to talk with me about the recent murder."

"I'm sorry, Miss—" David began before she interrupted.

"A-i-s-l-i-n-n," she spelled for him. "It is pronounced like ash-lynn."

"That's an interesting name." David smiled. "Is that Irish?"

"Yes, it is." She smiled a pleasing smile due to his recognition of her ancestry. "It is often mispronounced, so I have learned to just say 'Yes, that's me' when I hear people try to say it."

David laughed and found there to be something endearing about Aislinn as he felt himself enjoying her presence and heart-warming smile. He didn't feel the usual annoyance he felt as she tried to plead with him to share even a smidgeon of a detail as he had with many other reporters in the past, but he wasn't giving in. He could tell she was used to getting what she wanted, but not in an overconfident and arrogant way. She was one of those naturally pretty women who did not require any form of makeup to enhance their already attractive features. He figured her to be in her upper twenties and at ease with herself. She reminded him of one of those people you feel like you have known all your life after having just met them. David couldn't understand what it was about her that made him feel so at ease when he generally wasn't the talkative type. He could think of only one person who had ever made him feel like he could be completely himself and free of judgment, but she was gone now.

David was content to sit there and continue to talk, but the buzzing of his phone interrupted their opportunity to find out more about the other.

"Excuse me for a moment please," he asked before turning to take the call.

"Hough here," he spoke in the receiver. "I am on my way."

David turned back to Aislinn, disappointed he would not be able to continue their conversation. He glanced back up at her, and for a moment, there was something in her eyes which seemed vaguely but hauntingly familiar. He couldn't pinpoint exactly what it was, but it sparked some sort of vague memory.

"Is everything all right?" Aislinn asked, tilting her head and looking at him quizzically.

"Yes, I am sorry. I have to go," he lied as he continued to gaze into her green eyes. What he wanted to tell her is that her eyes are a rare green like he has never quite seen on the color spectrum and had the ability to extract anything from him as long as she continued to stare into his eyes, questioning where he had seen them before. "What's your last name, in the event I feel like talking about the case?"

"Cavanaugh." She smiled and offered him her business card before turning to exit the heavy transom door with the leaded stain glass that lead out to the sunlit sidewalk on the main street.

David motioned for his bill, and while getting a couple of dollars out to pay for his coffee, he placed her card in one of the open slots and took in a deep breath before walking into the sunlight and heading in the direction of his office. Traces of the previous nights' rain were still present along the street curbs and lower lying areas in the sidewalk, but they went unnoticed by him as he held his face toward the sun, hoping for a blast of light to shine down and miraculously lead him to the right path.

David had never cared for the character of the deceased prosecutor and knew he had history before David's time on the force, but he couldn't allow his feelings to interfere with his investigation. David had long since learned to handle business professionally and made it a point to never interact socially with any of his colleagues. He kept his private life just that, as well as protecting his family from work-related events. He felt there were some things he needed to shield them from so that his wife wouldn't worry. He strove for truth and justice daily and fought hard for programs for the youth in the area to provide them safe places and programs to instill character. If he had belief in karma, he would say this man certainly got what he had given many, but he still had to enforce the law no matter the crimes the prosecutor was known to have committed with no formal charges ever having been filed—a system designed to protect their own but penalize the remainder of society however they deemed necessary. David struggled internally with his feelings, but he also knew vigilante justice wasn't the right path, or they would be investigating far more murders than just the prosecutor's. David was a firm believer that law and order would inevitably prevail, but first those who were guilty of manipulating the system to their advantage would have to be brought to justice before proceeding with a fair and impartial system established to protect victims and those innocent of crimes they were falsely accused of. He often commented the system is quick to judge but, when in error, very slow to correct their wrongdoing. He did his best to do what he could every day in order to make not only his small town a better place, but he hoped it would spread its way also into the surrounding communities and continue until the whole of America stood proudly on their feet once again. His goal was to make the world a much better place for his son to grow into a healthy young man who would see more goodness in the world than the terrible things occurring daily around them and on the news.

CHAPTER 5

The sun shone warm on the stranger's skin as she knelt before the tombstone of Judge Nicholas Hallahan, whose remains had been buried in Saint Cecilia's Cemetery. A memorial plaque had been placed on the base of his ostentatious headstone commemorating his service to the community.

"I see they did not know you intimately as I had," the stranger began as she worked an engraving tool into the soft metal of the plaque. "You must have made some amends with God as he definitely showed you mercy by not providing me the opportunity to send you to hell personally after what you did to my family. It couldn't have been enough to make amends though, you sorry piece of shit. We'll see how your memory holds up once everyone knows the truth of what a demon you truly were."

The memories flooded her mind as she pressed harder into the metal and continued to talk aloud to the person she remembered as one of the men responsible for murdering her family. With a contorted face, twisted mouth, and bulging eyes lined with red from the tears that flowed as the memories spilled forth, she uttered each word with deliberate emphasis on certain words that described the hatred she felt in her heart for such a long time. Every day that she trained she would push herself to limits that no other human viewed possible, but she blocked her pain and pushed forward until she reached a satisfying goal in order to proceed with her plan, which had taken her years to formulate and initiate. Patience had been her friend, except in this particular circumstance she had been too late, she said aloud as she lifted her face toward the sky and laughed through her tears before stepping back to view her work. Satisfied she hadn't missed any details, she placed the tool back in its case and strolled the couple of blocks to Buccilli's Pizza and ordered a hot Italian sub and water with a twist of lemon before making her way to Pettit Park where she took a seat on the bench and watched the people, some of which she had perhaps once considered friends. She allowed her memories to take her back to the numerous times she had sat on this very same bench with her father. He would bring her to Tobacco River where they would fish for hours together to the chagrin of her mother. She laughed softly at the memory of her mother standing in the doorway with her arms crossed, reprimanding her father for taking their daughter to do things fathers do with their sons, warning him he was creating a tomboy rather than a young lady. Her father would take her mother in his arms and pull her close, telling her their daughter is as beautiful as she is, so he needed to teach her to defend herself.

She began to wonder if she had made the correct decision to return here as the fond memories of her father seemed to be making her weak, so she thought. In her eyes, he was very embodiment of what a father was—advisor, protector, teacher, and sometimes confidant. In other words, he was always her hero, setting the bar very high to compare against every man she met forever after. Her last memories would be the look of anguish on his face as he felt he had failed his family. She almost screamed aloud, "You tried, Daddy," before catching herself and leaning against the bench again.

Wiping the tears from her eyes, she stood and collected herself before departing down the path toward the town where she once strolled along the streets hand in hand with her mother. She would stop on occasion to look into the windows of the shops and recalled holidays past where the town was decorated for the festivities but continued her walk to McEwan Street to Cops and Doughnuts Bakery. It was a charming establishment where they make everything from scratch, and it is owned by the local police officers.

Ordering a coffee with her favorite hazelnut creamer, she took a seat near the window to feel the warmth of the sun shining through. The odd look she received from the cashier hadn't gone unnoticed, nor did the fact the woman scurried into the back before appearing in the doorway with another female of similar age. She didn't allow that to interfere with her thoughts of how she believed her father would love this place and would likely have been one of the owners. He was loved and well respected by everyone who knew him. He was one of the best officers this city had seen because of his loyalty to the citizens and his desire to keep the town family oriented. His devotion eventually cost him not only his life but also those of his beloved family. The people who truly knew her father didn't believe the story behind his death and the death of his family. The people behind murdering them made it appear her father had been involved in some illicit activities that got him and his family murdered, which left some of the citizens who had no firsthand knowledge of her family to believe the lies they built.

She wished she could hear what the two ladies were saying, but from the looks on their faces, she guessed they were being haunted with memories of her mother as they stared with no regard that she stared back at them as she listened intently to the locals chattering incessantly about the recent murder of the prosecutor and whispered softly to herself, "You haven't seen the best of it yet, folks. Hold on to your seats because the show has just begun."

CHAPTER 6

Aislinn took a seat at the bar in the Evening Post Bar and Grill and asked for their broasted chicken and tap beer. She was told by the locals how wonderful the food and atmosphere were and thought she would experience it for herself.

Taking a sip of her beer, she looked around the establishment to see if any of the faces looked familiar. Not recognizing anyone, she retrieved her tablet from her bag and powered it up. She was so engrossed in reading she didn't notice Detective Hough had entered and had taken the seat next to her until the bartender asked what he would like.

"I believe I will have what she is drinking," he advised before leaning in to ask Aislinn how her day had been.

"Hi. What a pleasant surprise," Aislinn replied, grinning from ear to ear. "I was just thinking about you."

"Oh, what have I done to warrant that?" David laughed, wondering why she would have a second thought about him.

"I was just thinking about the recent homicide and wondered if you've had any breaks in the case," Aislinn continued. "It isn't often prosecuting attorneys are murdered, especially in such a gruesome manner. Does it appear to be related to any recent cases?"

"How did you know the murder was gruesome and not just a regular shooting or stabbing?" David inquired. Leaning in closer, he awaited her reply.

"I am sure you have already figured that out." She smiled as she lifted her eyebrows to him. "It's a small town, and we all know secrets don't stay secrets long in these places."

"Then to answer your other question, that's what I am looking into, but there hasn't been any big cases as of late that would make any sense of what took place in that hotel room," David replied, tipping his beer and sipping the foam from the glass. "The message left by the murderer is even more confusing."

"What message is that?" Aislinn inquired.

"I really can't share the details, but it really makes no sense to me," David informed her while scratching his eyebrow with his little finger.

"Maybe if you could give me some idea, I could assist you in potentially making a connection," Aislinn prodded with a sly grin.

"Do you have any familiarity with the goddess Morrigan?" David asked. "It is connected with Irish folklore."

"I am very familiar with the Morrigan," Aislinn shared. "What does that have to do with the murder though?"

"I didn't say it was connected," David teased. "I may just want to know for myself."

"I see," Aislinn continued, playing along with David. "Morrigan is an Irish goddess, also known as Great Goddess in Europe. She's believed to be the transporter between life and death. She predates the Copper Age and is also known to have been a shape changer."

"I see you know your goddesses," David laughed.

"I am of Irish descent." Aislinn smiled before continuing, "I am certain you are aware of how the Irish love to tell their stories."

"Hence, you chose the journalism career?" David continued to tease. There was something about Aislinn which allowed him to feel at ease in her presence. He wasn't able to determine quite what it was, but he enjoyed the feeling it afforded him.

"I see you have quite the investigative skills," Aislinn began her own goading. "Those should come in handy."

David made a gesture of grabbing his heart and feigning injury, causing them both to chuckle before asking Aislinn to share more of what she knew about the goddess Morrigan. He listened intently as she continued the tale and described the many aspects of Morrigan. Many of the connections were made as Aislinn shared the more familiar character of King Arthur and how Morrigan and her two sisters played a role in his reign.

David didn't consider himself to be the scholarly type but was, in fact, highly intelligent. He had enjoyed reading some of the tales as a youth that Aislinn continued to describe. He had always had an easy time of school and tested in the genius range. David attended college right out of high school and had taken classics for prelaw and premed but discovered after taking a few classes he truly enjoyed investigative work and pursued his degree in criminal law and justice. He was aware he would never be rich in his career choice, but he was happy and content pursuing what he loved. Listening to Aislinn share her vast knowledge of literature and history, he was certain she was highly intelligent in her own right and enjoyed the animation in her voice as she shared what she had learned about the goddess Morrigan.

"Oh my, I must apologize to you for taking so much of your time," Aislinn expressed regretfully and was surprised herself that nearly two hours had passed as she shared what she thought may be important with David.

"No apology needed," David interrupted. "It has been a pleasure, and I hope to resume this conversation at a later date. Right now, I have a special little man awaiting me for his bedtime story, so I have to excuse myself."

"That's very admirable." Aislinn smiled. "I am sure he feels the same about his daddy. Have a great evening, Detective."

"You do the same, ma'am." David smiled in return before paying both his and Aislinn's tabs. "It's on me for the company."

Aislinn could envision David's family in her mind simply by the way he carried himself. She knew his mother was a loving and gracious person with high standards and morals and his father was similar character. He had a way about him which made one feel a genuine sense of ease and comfort in his presence. He reminded her much of her own father, whom she adored. David, from what she had discovered, was a trustworthy and thoughtful person. He appeared to be sincerely interested when she spoke, which meant a tremendous amount to Aislinn. She often felt she wasn't taken seriously for her work and mind because she was an absolutely beautiful young woman. She had inherited her mother's beautiful green eyes, tiny nose, and full mouth, but she had her father's charming smile and dark hair. She had her mother's slender figure but her father's height and could have taken the fashion industry by storm, but Aislinn had other pursuits in mind. Her mother had been sorely disappointed when Aislinn told her and her father she had made the decision to major in investigative journalism and criminology as her mother had pushed her in the direction of pursuing a career in film and modeling. She went on about how Aislinn was wasting her talents given her by God and how she was cheating the world of her beautiful voice. Aislynn enjoyed singing, but she had no desire to perform for a living. She was much more interested in educating her mind because it truly fed her soul. She was certain there was contention in her childhood home to this day since her father helped her to research schools which would provide her the education she desired and encouraged her to always be true to herself and her dreams.

Aislinn finished her meal and opened her tablet in hopes of getting some work done, but she found her thoughts strayed between childhood memories and those which wandered repeatedly back to the handsome detective. She had found him to be quite interesting, and she could tell that beneath the clothes he had a very fit physique. Normally she dismissed any thoughts of men because she still had goals she wanted to pursue without complicating them with a relationship, but David's charm had somehow managed to work its way into her soft spot, and she found herself wanting to know more about him without him knowing so he wouldn't feel she was a psycho stalker. She could still smell the scent of his cologne where he nonchalantly placed his hand in hers several times during their interaction this evening. Completely distracted by this discovery, she closed her tablet and left an extra tip since David had picked up her tab before walking into the cool evening air.

CHAPTER 7

"Aaaaggghh, you bitch. What did I do to you? Why are you doing this to me?" screamed Chief Haddy as he hung limp by his arms from the rafters of the dilapidated old cabin, his feet barely touching the ground, unable to defend himself from her attack. Each time she touched him with the probe, he would howl in pain as small foamy bubbles of spit would form in the corners of his clenched mouth as the electrodes shot through him. Wanting to watch him suffer, she decided to play mind games with him and found she felt powerful every time he would scream out in agony although she hadn't run the juice to the probe when touching him with it after shocking him several times prior. He would thrust against the chain, holding him in position at the reminder of the excruciating pain that shot down through every limb of his body and caused him to urinate down both his legs.

"You smell of piss, Chief, and you scream like a little girl," the stranger taunted, walking slowly around him as he dangled there weak and unable to move. "I didn't scream at all while you and your friends brutally assaulted me, did I, Chief Haddy?"

"What the hell are you talking about?" he spat, barely able to speak.

"Let me give you a little reminder then, shall I?" she replied, grabbing him by his hair and yanking his head up to look in her face as she removed the scarf covering her face with her other hand.

"You are dead." He choked the words as his eyes bulged from their sockets in disbelief. "I watched them kill you and put you in the ground. What the fuck is going on?"

"I believe that would have been my mother," she corrected him at the same time jabbing him several times in the ribs with her small but effective fists.

"But they killed you too," he continued when he was able to draw in a breath. "I saw them."

"No, you only thought they had after you and the others raped me one after another, leaving me beaten from resisting and bleeding from the trauma that destroyed my female reproductive system. I mean, most twelve-year-olds would have died from that attack, but not me. No, sir, not me," she continued, placing a collar around his neck and tightening it with each word she spoke. "I guarantee you that today you will definitely wish you and they had killed me because I plan to make you scream for a very, very long time. This is the very least of what I have planned for you. Imagine that and you are already crying. You are making this very fun for me, just so you know. Isn't that what you told me?"

"Fuck you, bitch!" he screamed and tried to spit in her face, but she jerked his head down with the leash, smashing his face roughly with her elbow.

"He has some fight left in him, does he?" she continued to mock

"You are dead, bitch, dead!" he screamed, trying to pull his legs from the ground to kick at her while she moved quickly and with ease from his reach. Each time he swung back, she would kick him directly in the abdomen, causing him to vomit down the front of himself.

"Aww, come on, Joe," she began. "The fun has only just begun. I have much more in store for you, only I am not certain you will enjoy it as much as I will. Isn't that what you told my father, Joe, as you shoved yourself inside of me and forced me to look at you while you did?"

She grabbed a rag close by and stuffed it in his mouth to stifle the screams she knew would be coming before she began removing his pants.

"I can't have you smelling like piss while I give you some of your own medicine now, can I, Joe?" She continued her taunting as she threw a bucket of cold water over him, and forcing each of his legs in a spread-eagle position, she secured them. Drawing a metal object she designed specifically for this moment from her bag, she told him exactly what she intended to do with it while running it up and down his abdomen and butt before jamming it repeatedly into his rectum and asking him if it felt good with each thrust as she relished in his agonized screams that sounded like muffled grunts and moans. She repeated every word to him he had said to her that day, and the stranger watched the light slowly ebb its way out from his eyes as he accepted he would not escape his fate.

"You sold your soul, Joe," she spoke, subsiding from her assault for the time being and removing the gag from his mouth. "You took a position to protect and uphold the law, yet you and the others saw monetary gain and chose to extort others through abuse of your power. You are worse than any criminal you helped imprison, but you are going to make it right, aren't you, Joe? You are going to answer every question I ask, and if you don't answer them honestly, Joe, you will force me to find your family, and I know you don't want that, Joe."

She sat on the floor next to him, intending to tape his answers as she grilled him for details and exact locations of the places she knew existed but had been unable to locate during her recent search.

"I want the exact location, Joe, of the girls you put in sex slavery," she demanded, reminding him she wasn't playing by punching him several times in the face before asking again. "You are also going to tell me the precise location of the meth labs you allow to operate here. I already know a few as I followed your dumb ass to them."

Joe hesitated before the reality of her words sunk in, and he sang like a canary in a coal mine. He, for a moment, thought she might take pity, but his arrogance and ignorance preceded any common sense the man could have.

"Your father should have kept his mouth shut, and none of that would have happened to you and your family. You should really be angry with him." Joe breathed heavily. "He should have taken the money and left, but he had to be an asshole and not mind his own business. He left us no choice."

"Each of you had a choice not to involve yourselves in criminal activity too," she interrupted with her correction of his belief, "especially when you took an oath to protect people. I'm here to right an injustice, Joe, that otherwise would have gone unpunished. The system is corrupt and blind, so I'd rather not involve them in our affairs. I am quite adept at seeking my own justice, and it won't cost me a dime in comparison to the exorbitant fees charged by attorneys. It's much simpler this way. An eye for an eye, Joe."

"You're dead, bitch." He laughed insanely. "You are dead. They will find you and finish you once and for all just like your weak father. He watched instead of doing anything to protect you and your family. He knew you all were at risk, yet he did nothing to protect you. Oh, they will find you, you fucking cunt! They will find you!"

"I can assure you that I will be long gone before your rotting corpse is found along with the others," she mocked, forcing the gag back into his mouth. "It will take them time to put it together. After all, everyone believes that I am dead, so I may have to leave a few extra bread crumbs. Then again, Detective Hough is actually detective material and has half a brain, so he may just figure it out before I finish. One fact remaining, he didn't figure it out before I got to you."

Joe collapsed against the restraints and lost consciousness briefly from the continued assault to his rectum, disappointing the stranger, as she had expected more from a man of his stature and physique.

She had suddenly lost interest and had no desire to hear more from him, so she prepared to finish what she had come to do. Initially, she wanted to take her time and listen to him beg for his miserable life, but now she was ready to finish her task. Removing the fillet knife from its case, she proceeded to carve him in the same manner he and the others had her mother, watching as his bloodshot eyes grew large and his face twisted in pain. She watched as the last ember of light faded from his eyes and his dying body thrust forward, giving one final exhale.

"You are very disappointing, Joe," she spat in anger, slumped against his already stiffening corpse. "My mother withstood more than you could."

She dipped the end of the pen in the pool of blood surrounding his body and wrote, "Ta an cath a bhuaigh beagnach. Go gairid, beidh an fiach dubh curtha dioahaltar," meaning, "The battle has almost been won. Soon, the raven will have been avenged."

Taking a few moments to check her work before cleaning the cabin of any trace of her, she looked around once more before gathering her remaining things and closed the door behind her. Following the trail through the woods, she made her way along the moonlit footpath. She had surveyed it several times, counting her footsteps to certain key locations throughout the woods since it would be very dark during the night and difficult to find your way with low lighting. She had followed him numerous times in order to learn his routine. That's how she was able to locate some of the meth labs he and the others were running, and she kept good logs so that law enforcement could easily locate them once she released the information to them. He had become too confident in their schemes and wasn't paying attention.

Retrieving the motorbike from the brush, she secured the items to the back and drove the path back several miles to the main road before cutting off onto another trail twenty miles up the road where her father's cabin sat. She secured the bike in the storage shed behind the cabin and retrieved the spare key from its usual hiding place and unlocked the door, pushing it open as it groaned against her force, not having been opened for some years. The hinges squeaked as the door swung wider, and she stepped inside. She gazed around the cabin and was surprised to find everything as she had remembered. The place needed a good dusting, but it wasn't as bad as she had expected considering the time frame which had passed since her last visit.

"This was one of your favorite places, Dad," she whispered aloud, picking up a framed photo of her and her father on the stand next to the entry and wiping the light layer of dust from the glass. "You really gave us some great memories in this place."

Setting the frame back in its exact spot, she walked toward the door which led to her parents' bedroom in the cabin and slowly turned the handle, sighing deeply before pushing the door completely open.

She walked to the bed and sat on the edge as she had so many times as a child and reached toward her father's robe which still hung from a rack of a deer mounted on the wall. Lifting the material to her face, she smelled it and thought she could almost smell a faint hint of his scent on the robe. Tossing the cover of the bed back, she climbed in and wrapped herself in the robe. She needed to hold on to anything that kept her memories of her father's smell, the sound of his voice, and laughter alive as she thought she was beginning to lose the sound of his voice and the way he always smelled like a crisp fall day to her. She had always been told by others that you often lose those as a way to move on from the pain of losing your loved ones, but she didn't ever want to lose those memories as they were the best of her life.

CHAPTER 8

"Good morning, Mr. Sun," Aislinn called to the sun as she stretched and smiled, reaching for her robe near the foot of the bed. She slipped it around her and slid her feet over the edge of the bed, stretching them to find her slippers. "I think it looks like a glorious day."

She walked to the kitchen and started the coffee before turning the dial on the shower to the perfect temperature she enjoyed and stepping beneath the tiny streams of water pouring from the shower spout. She smiled as she thought about the things she would see today. She had spoken with some of the locals and made a list of things she wanted to visit while she was there. She was excited to explore Shingle Lake and to have an opportunity to enjoy nature but wanted to stop by Clare Sweet Shop on the way and pick up a couple of items she felt she absolutely had to try.

Dressed in casual capris and a T-shirt, she pulled her hair into a ponytail, dabbed on a light shade of lipstick, and strolled out the door into the sunshine. Placing her handbag in the basket on her bicycle, she pedaled her way through the streets of Clare to the sweet shop. She parked her bicycle off to the side and entered the glass-paned door beneath the awning and allowed her nose to enjoy the heavenly scent from all the sweets that surrounded her. Undecided, she continued to browse around the little shop when she heard a familiar voice and turned to see David entering the door with a little boy she presumed to be his son. She smiled at him and was amused to see how much the little boy resembled him.

"I see you do have a knack for finding all the good places," David began. "Aislinn, I would like you to meet my son, Gabe. Gabriel, this is Aislinn."

Aislinn's heart melted when he reached his little hand toward hers to shake and told her he was pleased to meet her and flashed a smile which was sure to win him the attention of many young ladies.

"What an absolute darling he is!" Aislinn exclaimed as Gabriel made his way to the counter where the clerk smiled and waited to talk with him until he had made his way comfortably into her lap.

David explained he had brought him here since he was old enough to enjoy sweets, and it was evident he was deeply loved by the owners of the shop. He and Gabriel would make the weekly trip as part of their uninterrupted father-son time. He explained that he would allow Gabriel to pick the activities for the day, and naturally, this place made the list each time. He believed his son was blessed to have so many wonderful people show so much love for his child after he lost his mother. David was fond of many of the residents in the community and grateful they were a part of their lives. He was sure it aided in Gabriel's ability to understand and accept the loss of his mother. He told her it was Gabriel who often had the wise words for him when his son recognized his father's pain.

Aislinn giggled to break the ice because she struggled seeing the pain that remained in his eyes when he spoke of his wife. She told David she could understand why this would always be on his list as she was still undecided as to which treats she would allow herself today.

"You can never go wrong with these," David encouraged, pointing to the turtles. "I believe they are the best I've ever had."

"I am going to trust your taste on this one," Aislinn caved and decided to go with David's suggestion. "These will be great while riding around Shingle Lake."

"Shingle Lake!" Gabriel exclaimed, running back in the direction of his father. "I want to go to Shingle Lake, Dad. Can we go with you?"

"Hold on there, big guy," David began as he picked Gabriel up in his arms. "First of all, I thought you said earlier you wanted to go to a movie, and secondly, it was not very polite of you to invite yourself that way."

"I'm sorry, ma'am," Gabriel apologized in a soft voice, putting his head down against his father's chest as his lower lip began to protrude.

"Apology accepted, and I would love to have you join me, if your father agrees," Aislinn consoled him without making it appear she was in disagreement with David. She felt a parent should not be undermined when they are teaching their children morals and respect. Her heart melted at Gabriel's sweet apology, but his disappointment at possibly not going was more than she could bear to see from such a darling young man. He still had some of his baby face left, but you could begin to see some of his boyish features beginning to appear.

"Can we go, Daddy?" Gabriel pleaded, interrupting her thoughts of the idea that if she had a son, she would want him to look just like this bundle of joy.

"We will have to go back and get our bikes," David explained. "That would take about thirty minutes, if you would like to wait."

"She can put her bike on the rack of the Jeep and ride with us to get ours," Gabriel explained, looking up at his dad with his big hazel eyes.

"I suppose if Ms. Aislinn would like to take a ride with us, I am good with that." David seemed to almost stutter the words, oblivious that the store owner had been observing their interaction with a big smile covering her face. "Let me get these for you," David asked, holding his hands out to receive the candy turtles with a smile stretching from one ear to the other. "This way, if you don't agree they are the best, then you will have lost nothing." Aislinn handed him the candy and followed him and Gabriel to the Jeep and stood back as he opened the passenger door for her to climb in. "We could put the bikes on the back and drive over if you like."

"I would enjoy the company," Aislinn agreed and joined Gabriel in David's jeep while he loaded her bike onto the back rack.

Gabriel talked incessantly to Aislinn during the drive, and David was unable to get a word in edgewise. He was amused by Gabriel's immediate attraction to Aislinn. He had only seen him behave in this manner with Ms. Mary and the clerks in the candy shop. It was obvious Gabriel felt the same sense of comfort with Aislinn as he had. She was most definitely an amazingly beautiful woman, but she had an earthiness about her, which made her easily approachable. It appeared Aislinn was enjoying the company as much as Gabriel. David felt a comfort he hadn't experienced in several years, and it unsettled him yet somehow rejuvenated him. He was relieved when they arrived at his home and he could get away to breathe for a few minutes while getting his and Gabriel's bikes. Aislinn seemed to overwhelm his senses, but it wasn't because she was trying. She was simply being herself.

Gabriel was happy to show Aislinn around their house and introduced her to Ms. Mary. Their Irish wolfhound, Chompy, even took immediately to her as he planted his head in her lap while she chatted with Ms. Mary, his tail wagging with each pat she gave his head.

"We should probably be on our way if we want to enjoy the warmth the sun offers," David suggested as he rose from the over-stuffed leather chair to open the door for them. "It can get pretty cool in the evenings here."

Aislinn said her goodbyes to Ms. Mary and took the hand Gabriel offered and walked through the door with him while David closed it behind him. David followed them around the Jeep and, once again, opened the door for Aislinn and Gabriel before climbing in the driver's side.

David shared much of his knowledge about the nature that surrounded them, driving at a leisure speed. He would pull over after spotting a few eagles or an occasional osprey and would point them out to her and Gabriel during their drive to the lake. He was explaining how an osprey dives down to catch the fish so that she might capture a photo, but as he said it, the bird flew down and tucked its wings and came back up with a fish between its talons. It was an exciting moment for everyone although Aislinn was unable to react that quickly with her camera not in reach. They all laughed at the situation and missed opportunity.

The peace and beauty of the environment offered them the opportunity to relax, which, in turn, relaxed their topics of conversation. They shared things about themselves, and each was as surprised as the other to discover they had many similar interests.

David was utterly in awe when Aislinn shared she had studied forensic science but decided she preferred investigative journalism. She explained she felt she could better inform the public with the truth in matters, which otherwise appear to be swept under the rug, depending on the individuals involved. She felt that well-informed people have an opportunity to make decisions based on actual facts that are oftentimes twisted to be made misleading in nature. This quality impressed upon his logical side further, and he appreciated that she was able to express her thoughts in a manner which piqued the interest of others.

David was able to relate to a certain degree with her belief in the system as he had seen special favors done for similar behaviors and acts, which, most likely, would have landed any other citizen behind bars and an appearance in court. If any charges were incurred, they were never made public so those privileged wouldn't have their names tainted. Is this really fair in a system of justice and equality for all?

Aislinn enjoyed listening to David share his childhood memories of having grown up in the Holland area. She had always enjoyed her family trips there to visit during the Tulip Times Festival. The town was always so alive with happy people wandering the shops, breweries, and cafés in the area. She remembered the town was always so clean and inviting, and it appeared they took pride in their community, which, to her, spoke of the strong family values, which she explained she believes has taken a major downward spiral in other communities that may take years to rebound from. She was in no way saying that it was free of crime because no city has that luxury, but she felt a sort of friendliness about the place.

David shared with her that he and his wife met while they were in college. They had transferred to Clare after they both graduated and he and his wife married. She had grown up in the area, and her extended family all lived within proximity to one another. David enjoyed the nature, so he wasn't reluctant to move to please his wife.

Her love for her family was part of the reason he had fallen so in love with her.

Their conversation was a variety of topics, and Aislinn laughed as he shared some of the antics he pulled on his parents growing up, but he would whisper so as not to allow Gabriel to hear. She felt from his description she knew them intimately and thought his parents sounded like angels. It was apparent to her that David had high regard for them both, and he explained he would visit as often as he could in order for Gabriel to have an opportunity to have exposure to the same environment he grew up in. They would generally head down for a long weekend at least once a month, and Gabriel would sleep in David's old room. His mother had kept it just as it was when he was a child living under their roof and was proud to share with Gabriel each of his father's awards and how she could remember as if it were yesterday.

"Aislinn, I have something for you," Gabriel interrupted with a beaming smile as he held out a handpicked bouquet of wildflowers to her.

"Oh, my goodness, sweetie! Thank you!" Aislinn exclaimed as her smile reflected in her eyes. "These are the most beautiful flowers I have ever received."

Her compliment made his smile even brighter, and he proudly looked at his father and winked. David couldn't resist the temptation to boost Gabriel's esteem higher by telling him he certainly has excellent taste in women and is very wise to have picked an educated woman such as Aislinn to court. Gabriel gave him a high five and skipped back toward the lake to throw rocks.

"I have been outdone by a miniature Cassanova." David laughed. "I am not sure if I can outdo such beauty."

"Let me see if I have any napkins in my pack so that I can wet them and put the flowers in until I can get them in a vase." Aislinn smiled. "You will have to be creative to outdo that little man."

"I can certainly provide you with this empty water bottle as a makeshift vase," David offered while feigning humility. "I understand it detracts from the beauty of the flowers for the time being, but it will help them keep their luster."

They both laughed and made their way to where Gabriel stood throwing stones across the water to make them skip along until they lost their speed and sunk in the depths of the lake. David bent to put water in the bottle so Aislinn could preserve them for now. Filling it halfway, he handed it to her to place the flowers.

David picked up a few stones himself and joined Gabriel in creating ripples on the water. The kerplunk sound the rocks made on their final skip across the water, and the birds singing were the only sounds Aislinn could hear as she stood and watched them together. She decided to join them and took a spot next to Gabriel where there were smaller stones along the water's edge. She observed as Gabriel would watch David's technique and try to replicate his moves. She giggled inside since Gabriel was already the image of his father, with the exception of his eyes. She presumed he must have inherited his mother's warm hazel eyes with flecks of gold around the pupil that made the green brighter.

"Gabriel, stop!" Aislinn shouted and lunged toward him, startling both him and David.

David grabbed Gabriel and stood in disbelief as he watched Aislinn standing there with a snake dangling from her right hand. She had caught it just behind the head as it struck at Gabriel. David quickly examined Gabriel to see if it had bitten him anywhere before turning back to Aislinn, who was now at the water's edge, trying to untangle the snake from her arm to release it a safe distance from where they were.

"That was truly amazing," David stuttered, setting Gabriel back on the ground, and taking the end of the snake, he began unwinding it. "I have never seen anything like it before. How did you do that? I am more than impressed."

"I wasn't able to recognize that it was just a harmless Nerodia sipedon, otherwise known as northern water snake. They aren't poisonous, but they will bite if they feel threatened," she calmly explained. "I guess I saw a threat, and my instincts kicked in."

David stood there just staring at her with what he felt had to have been the most ridiculous facial expression. He couldn't even speak, let alone grasp, that she had reacted without fear in a situation most women would have run from and then to completely baffle him with the exact specie of snake. *Would this woman ever fail to astonish me?* he asked himself.

"Why are you looking at me like that?" Aislinn inquired. "I apologize for startling Gabriel."

"No, it isn't that," David began. "I have just never seen anything like it before. You were like some ninja warrior without the black clothing."

"I will have to share that with my trainer," Aislinn teased as she called Gabriel over to where they were about to release the snake. She wanted him to see the snake and explained what kind of snake it was before telling him the snake was actually afraid of him and thought he was going to harm it. She explained that its defense is to bite, but the most enlightening thing she explained to Gabriel was that he should always be aware of his surroundings at all times. She didn't want him to be afraid of snakes, so she asked him if he would like to touch it before she allowed it to swim away. David was impressed at how she handled the situation and prevented Gabriel the pain caused by a bite, as well as a day spent at the ER.

They stood there by the edge and watched as the snake swam away, happy that the day was able to continue well. Aislinn suggested they retrieve the basket from her bicycle and enjoy a nice picnic lunch. She laid out a red-and-white checkered cloth for them to sit on as she fondly remembered her mother doing during her childhood. She pulled several containers from her cool pack, along with a traveling picnic case which held plates, silverware, napkins, two glasses, and miniature salt and pepper shakers. Aislinn prepared a plate for Gabriel and set it in front of him before asking David what he would like.

"I believe I will try a little of everything." David smiled although his insides seemed to be shaking. She was having this effect on him he hadn't even felt with his wife whom he loved deeply. There was something so intriguing about her that kept him excited and alive feeling, anticipating his next discovery of her many facets. He felt as though she truly understood the beauty of life and cherished it, as if the fate of the world depended on it.

Aislinn retrieved her camera and shared some shots with David she had taken of him and Gabriel earlier by the lake. She wanted to surprise him with some framed shots, but she liked them so much herself she couldn't wait. David was clearly moved by his emotions as she shared each picture. He felt she had managed to capture their thoughts and emotions in each frame.

"Your work is some of the best I have seen, Aislinn," David complimented. "You have an ability to capture a precise moment and have it tell so much to the viewer. How did you get to be so amazing? I really need to know."

"Now look who is teasing." Aislinn smiled and her embarrassment showed as her cheeks turned a deep shade of pink, and she replied modestly, "I can only capture what the lens sees. Photos, in a way, are a sort of truth and can tell you a lot about that person if you look close enough. I think most people are pretty easy to read. You just have to make certain that you remain aware and always look into their eyes. The eyes are the window to the soul and reveal things most people have no clue about."

"Humility is attractive on you," David replied softly. "Now please just take the compliment and accept that you are exceptional."

"Thank you, Detective. I will take that into consideration." Aislinn shot him a dazzling smile before turning to Gabriel to see if he needed anything else. It was clear he was finished as he had taken a couple of his matchbox cars from his pocket and used the cloth as a track to race them. Aislinn cleared the remaining food from the plates and placed everything in a plastic bag before putting it back in the carrier to wash later.

"It's getting late, so we should probably start back," David suggested. "It can get pretty cool here after the sun goes down, and I figure we have about an hour back to the Jeep, which should be perfect timing."

Gabriel had discovered a new supply of energy and talked about how much he enjoyed the day and wants to learn more about snakes so he can catch one like Aislinn did. She and David laughed quietly at his newfound braveness and said they would love to learn more about them too.

"Thank you, gentlemen, for a lovely day," Aislinn said as she exited the Jeep and waited for David to hand her bicycle to her from the rack. "I had a really great time."

"The pleasure is mine, ma'am," David replied with a slight bow of his head. "Thank you again for saving the day with the ninja move. I am still mind boggled over that."

Aislinn laughed and shook her head as she pushed the bike through the gate entrance toward her cottage. She turned for another glance and smiled a radiant smile as she waved good night to them before proceeding down the path to her cottage. David stood watching until she was out of sight.

CHAPTER 9

"Where is that piece of shit?" the stranger asked, pacing back and forth behind the row of arborvitaes which lined the yard, providing a sense of privacy for the tenant. Her agitation grew more intense, but she tried not to pace too much to prevent leaving any worn-down patches. "He is always here by this time."

Her hands trembled as she tried to hide the flame from the lighter as she inhaled the smoke from her fourth cigarette since her arrival. She was careful to place them in a baggie so that she did not leave any traces of her presence. Leaning against the tree, she took a long draw from the cigarette cupped in her hand and exhaled it, letting out a long stream of smoke. She closed her eyes and listened carefully for any sign of someone else or for the car she awaited to pull in the drive.

She had thought about these circumstances for a very long time as she trained for just these moments. Many times she ran other scenarios through her head regarding the people involved in the murder of her family and how she should proceed with getting justice for her loved ones. She had hoped in a system her father had taught her was good and righteous but was sadly disappointed when she witnessed their brutal murders by those who swore to protect and honor their fellow mankind. This was not to be the case as she had a strong feeling they would escape any punishment by their fellow peace officers and lawmakers. Her belief in the justice system was decimated by their acts and validated her in seeking her own justice. She pondered how many others' lives had been destroyed in the same fashion by these ingrates and murderers. Investigator Todd Ball was not going to escape with his life either, she mused as she heard the hum of the motor coming down the street and watched the headlights as they shone around the sides of the garage. She could hear the opening and closing of the garage door followed by the side entry door to his home.

Her fury grew as she thought of the many others who had been railroaded into charges concocted by these soulless creatures for their own financial gain or other families destroyed in a similar fashion as her own. She could have been as heartless as they had been and executed their family members along with them, but she thought that would make her just like the very monsters she came to destroy, and that is not what she wanted. Instead, she learned when her victims would be alone and chose to remove them from any environment they might be discovered by their family.

Stepping out of the shadows cast by the streetlamp, she made her way toward the house and stepped up on the porch, pausing momentarily to prepare herself completely before reaching out and ringing the doorbell, confident he had had time to get inside his home. Listening for any sounds from the other side, she leaned in and rang it once again.

"I will be right there." She heard his voice on the other side before hearing the door unlock and the slight sound of the seal of the door releasing as it opened. "Can I help you?"

"Hi, yes, I certainly hope so." She began reaching out to hold the storm door as she proceeded. "I am looking for a friend's house, and I am afraid I have gotten myself turned around."

"Sure, what street are you looking for?" he asked.

"She said she lives on Cottage Avenue, but I have been unable to find the address, and it ends at the cemetery," the stranger continued.

"She must live on the other side of the cemetery where Cottage Avenue picks up again. You can get to it by crossing down to Schoolcrest Avenue," he explained before turning to proceed back inside the door, planning to close it as he felt he had given her direction.

"Is there another way where I don't have to pass by both cemeteries?" she inquired, causing him to pause, and he watched as she changed her expression to reflect one of fear and concern.

"There is, but it is pretty dark and you will still have to pass one of them either way you choose to go," he explained, trying once again to close the door, but she again placed her hand on it and continued.

"I definitely had my friend drop me off at the wrong end then." She laughed nervously. "Is there any possibility that I could inconvenience you for a ride just past the cemetery and I can take it from there?"

"I don't suppose that would hurt anything." He hesitated before laughing along and telling her to meet him in the drive and he would get his car.

"That would be great." She smiled shyly, stepping from the porch and walking toward the drive where she waited at the end of the sidewalk for him to pull the car from the garage. Aislinn walked around the vehicle and slid into the passenger seat.

"I really appreciate the ride." She feigned embarrassment at her pretend fear of the cemetery. "Those places just really give me the creeps."

"That's because people are dying to get in there." Ball made an attempt at a joke decades old. "Are you from around here?"

"I once was, but there is nothing here for me anymore," she replied.

"Then why would you come here?" Ball inquired, continuing his attention on the road.

"As I said earlier, I do still have some friends in the area, so maybe I should have phrased it different," she corrected. "I also have some unfinished business I need to take care of, and you are a part of that."

"What are you talking about?" he asked, hitting the brakes to his car.

"Keep driving," she warned him, showing him the gun she had aimed at him in her pocket.

Investigator Ball picked speed back up and followed the directions she gave him and told him not to try anything else or she would not hesitate shooting him.

"What is this all about?" he asked nervously before proceeding to ask her if it was about money and telling her they could take care of that right now, and he would give her everything he had in his wallet.

She sat there silently, ignoring his plea, and wouldn't speak until she told him when and where to turn.

"Now turn off your lights and pull down this road," she told him. "Pull in over there and shut off the car."

"Where are we going?" he asked again.

"Just shut up and do what I tell you," she warned through clenched teeth and ordered him out of the car once the car came to a stop. She made him follow her close to the water's edge and ordered him to bend and retrieve the pair of oars on the shore before telling him to get in the boat that had been tied off close by.

The investigator rowed across the water with no idea what awaited him.

CHAPTER 10

Aislinn woke from the sun shining through the tiny cracks in the blinds and was surprised to see that she had slept until nearly eight o'clock the following morning as she had always been an early riser. She stretched her body and yawned before retrieving her robe at the foot of the bed where she had left it that night. She made her way to the bathroom and splashed some cool water over her face and headed to the kitchen to start a pot of coffee, which she normally didn't drink, but it was obvious to her that she needed the extra energy boost.

Making her way back to the bedroom, she picked up her phone from the nightstand and nearly dropped it when she saw she had missed several calls and text messages from David. Without reading any of the messages she pressed the Call button since she felt a sense of urgency on his behalf.

"Hi, David, it's me, Aislinn," she started when she heard his voice on the other end. "My phone was on silent, so it didn't wake me when you phoned. What's up?"

She listened as David explained his reason for calling and apologized for having called her so many times, but the urgency of the matter only allowed him a window of time to get what he wanted and asked if she would be willing to meet him.

"Absolutely, but are you sure I am the right person for this?" Aislinn asked. Grabbing a pen and paper from the bedside drawer, she began jotting down the directions as he explained them to her. Confirming the directions, she told him she would be about half an hour. She made a mad dash for the bathroom after hanging up for a quick shower. Turning the shower dial to warm, Aislinn stepped

48

into the shower and barely towel dried before slipping into her clothing and opting for a ponytail so she didn't have to spend time dealing with her naturally curly hair. She applied mascara and lip gloss, grabbed her keys and the directions, and headed out the door. She typed in the location David had given her, and it appeared to be taking her up near Lake Shamrock. He requested she meet him at the end of Shamrock Boulevard where it appears the road ends. He suggested she message him shortly before arriving so he could be right there in order to keep her from having to wait. She followed the GPS until she knew she was only a couple of blocks away and turned it off to message him. She made the right turn onto Shamrock and drove the length of the road slowly so she wouldn't pass by him. Aislinn caught sight of David stepping out from behind a grove of trees and waved for her to keep pulling forward. She turned the engine off to the car, and he was already there opening her door and helping her to step out.

"Thanks for coming, Aislinn," David greeted her. "I really don't want to ask you to do this, but I really need your expertise with something."

"What is it, David?" Aislinn asked.

"I need you to help me translate something," he began. "But what you will have to see is pretty gruesome, and there is no way for me to protect you from that. I will have to remind you, though, that you are not permitted to speak with anyone besides myself about anything that you may see or hear pertaining to what you are about to witness."

"I understand as it is a crime scene, but may I remind you also that I have seen a lot, David," Aislinn explained. "This is what all my training and education has been about. I believe I can handle this."

"Did you bring your camera?" David asked, hoping she had remembered. "You will probably want to get some photos of the scene in order to transcribe the words to English."

"I never go anywhere without at least one." She smiled, opening the trunk of her car and showing him her camera equipment. She handed him her tripod and gathered what she felt she would need and then followed him down a short path to the edge of the water where they would take a boat over to a small island in the middle of the lake.

David helped Aislinn into the fishing boat, and they traveled the short distance to the island where he docked on shore as near the crime scene as he could. He had explained to her on the way he needed her to see if she could translate the words for him and take photos of the scene as she sees it. He felt she could get a better feeling for what took place over any of the others he worked with, and her photos would be much better quality.

"Are you sure you are ready for this?" David asked once again, still feeling anguished about exposing her to something which would forever be a memory etched in her delicate mind. There was a part of her which assured him she could handle it, but there was a side to Aislinn which reminded him of the innocence he saw in his son. There was a pureness to her that he didn't see in many women her age in today's society.

"I've got this, David. I promise," she assured him while taking his hand to step from the boat, careful to not drop any of her equipment in the water. She followed him to a shelter where she could see several people, some observing the crime scene while others stood in small groups drinking coffee and discussing their opinions of what happened. She glanced around her to orient herself in direction before stepping closer with David to see the body. Without saying anything, she took out her camera and began photographing the inscriptions on the body first from different angles, at times zooming in to get the details of the inscription carved deep into the flesh of the corpse, which now appeared gray in color from loss of blood. She took several more shots of the victim before shooting the pavement in front of where his body laid spread-eagle and nearly quartered, stiff against the concrete, still bound by the ropes which prevented his escape from his abductor.

"Are you able to make out what it says?" David asked quietly when it appeared she was nearly satisfied with her work after having taken numerous close-up shots of the body.

"I want to take a closer look once I see these on the screen so that I can be certain," Aislinn replied, continuing to photograph the area. "I can make out parts clearly, but some of it is questionable. I think if I can take it from several angles, I will be able to read it much clearer. Just a few more shots and I will be ready to go."

"Do you mind if I join you while you work on it?" David asked, outstretching his hand to help her with her equipment. "I have found that two heads can be better than one most times, especially when your partner is very bright."

"I am comfortable with that." Aislinn smiled, handing him some of her equipment and following him back to the boat. "I really tried to get the best shots like I was trained to do, but shooting fake crime scenes are a lot different than the real thing."

"I understand because I have honestly never seen anything like these murders, but I felt you handled it like a pro," David stated, taking her equipment first and securing it before helping her in the boat once again.

"Thank you." Aislinn smiled, taking her seat and maintaining her balance as the boat rocked with the small waves. "I always at least attempt to try to do the things I don't think I can sometimes. That's the only way we know our capabilities."

"I couldn't agree with you more, and now I find myself needing to ask another favor," David began with a sheepish grin on his face. "I forgot that I didn't drive. Is there a possibility that I might get a lift from you?"

Aislinn grinned and pretended to ponder the thought before telling him it wasn't a problem since they would be reviewing the photos together. With that, she handed off the remainder of her equipment for him to carry so that she could fish her keys from her handbag. Locating them, she unlocked the doors and released the trunk latch to place her equipment safely in the compartments she had designed to protect it from theft or possible damage.

"Is this the new BMW i8?" David asked, having gotten a better look at her car than he had earlier upon her arrival. He was clearly impressed by the features of the car although he generally wasn't interested in such things.

"It is," Aislinn confirmed with a nod, pressing a button to close the trunk as David continued to walk around the car.

"I don't know if I should even ride in your car. You keep it so spotless," David complimented while looking down at his feet to see if he had mud on his shoes from docking the boat. "I don't want to be the first to get it dirty."

"I am, by no means, gentle on this machine." Aislinn laughed to make him at ease. "Besides, it has floor mats and washes."

"You must really be very good at what you do to get paid so well in your career," David commented. "I am estimating around $160,000 for this beauty."

"You are very close." Aislinn smiled without providing him the numbers. She asked if he would like to drive, extending her hand and offering him the key, which was nothing but a small square box with buttons.

"You're a saint," David teased. Realizing it was a keyless start, he handed it back to her and climbed in the seat behind the wheel and admired the interior. "Whoa, what's it doing?"

"It's adjusting to your driving needs, or you can choose your own comfort," Aislinn explained as the car continued to make the proper adjustments.

"I can see why you chose this one." David smiled in agreement of her choice and placed the car in drive. He was clearly enjoying the feel of the car and its rapid acceleration. Aislinn explained she enjoyed the comfort it provided for the long drives she takes, and he couldn't have agreed with her more. "You certainly keep it in impeccable condition."

"I was taught to take care of the people and things you're given in life," Aislinn explained. "I was taught that if you show them respect, in turn they will respect you, but that is not always the case either, Detective. If only people understood this concept and worked harder at it. Nowadays some people want everything handed to them, but they don't want to put any effort into its care or maintenance, be it fellow mankind, pets, or material objects. If it doesn't meet their expectations, they readily get rid of it or ignore it. We live in a throwaway world where nothing is valued, not even people and relationships."

"I agree that describes a large portion of humanity, but I believe there are more good people who want the same things you mentioned. They just don't know how to go about obtaining it," David contradicted, continuing to enjoy the drive. "It's unfortunate the press usually only covers the bad news and that people feed from the negativity. Imagine waking to the news, telling us about random acts of kindness instead of tragedy that took place locally or in another location."

"Hmmm, I suppose my perspective could be somewhat skewed since this is what I usually cover," Aislinn pontificated before continuing. "I have seen the worse humanity has to offer, and I am certain you have seen your share as well. That has a tendency to taint your vision on occasion."

"I have seen the aftermath of many atrocities, but I can also see the good," David began. "I try not to allow the bad things to overshadow the good since I have so much to be thankful for in this life."

"Yes, having someone to be thankful for and who brightens your day definitely changes the playing field," Aislinn replied casually as she fidgeted in the seat, suddenly uncomfortable with their conversation topic.

David could visibly see the change the conversation had over Aislinn. He didn't wish to make her feel anything but happy as he enjoyed the smile that lit her face, but he wanted to know what made her so tense and unsettled. Choosing not to pursue the subject further for now, he began asking her questions about her childhood and her family in which she appeared even more elusive.

Aislinn wanted to kick herself as she continued to squirm around and look for something to distract her. *This man has the ability to read me like no other, and I can't control my emotions with him*, she thought to herself, trying to regain her composure before distracting him with questions of her own.

David smiled a half-crooked smile, recognizing her tactics and rolling along with what made her comfortable; after all, he was, in a large sense, a stranger to her, so he kept his end of the conversation casual for the remainder of the drive. He pulled her car in front of her cottage and handed her the keys before helping her retrieve the items she needed from the trunk. David allowed her to lead the way down the path to the cottage, and she unlocked the door with her free hand and invited him inside. He smiled as he looked around at the quaint vintage decor of the interior. The walls were painted in pastels, and the furnishings were Victorian. The tables and built-ins were laced in doilies with porcelain knickknacks and vases of flowers adorning them. The entire space was bright and airy, giving one a sense of cheeriness and well-being, but certainly feminine in taste.

"This side of you surprises me somewhat," David teased. "I had you figured more of the modern style with all of your traveling. You know, easy to maintain and less to worry with."

"There are many aspects of me which would surprise you, Detective, but let's just say I enjoy getting in touch with the feminine side on occasion. It makes life more interesting that way," Aislinn teased back as she loaded the card from her camera to her laptop so they could review the photos she took of the crime scene.

David found himself wanting to know much more than she was ready to share. In fact, he wanted to know everything about her. He felt that she had somehow bewitched him, and he desperately needed to know what made her smile with happiness, like the day they spent at the lake. She appeared to be relaxed and content in that environment, less on guard and rigid, as she portrayed herself now. He thought it could be possible she is more serious when she works in order to remain focused, and he hoped seeing the gruesome sight of the corpse earlier hadn't traumatized her. He watched as she closely examined each photo that uploaded on the screen. He knew without the aid of Google Translate, he would have to try to copy each word exactly as it appeared on the body, but with Aislinn, she was able to read it with no problem. What couldn't be inscribed into the flesh of the body was written out on the floor of the gazebo in the victim's blood. He remained silent in his observation of her work and knew she had translated its entirety when he saw a glint of light take spark in her eyes. She looked up at him and tilted her head to the side before explaining there were a couple of areas which could interpret a couple different ways, so she wanted to be certain both made sense to him or one made more sense.

"Could you give me just a minute to make a call please?" David asked apologetically, asking to excuse himself from the room.

"Absolutely, it's no problem," Aislinn assured him. "Feel free to step in the parlor and close the door if you need privacy."

"Thank you." David smiled, making his way to the parlor. "I will only be a few minutes. I need to call Mary."

Aislinn wasn't trying to listen to his conversation, but she was able to overhear it in the small space. She smiled inside listening to him talk with Gabriel and how sorry he was he wouldn't be there to read to him tonight but that Ms. Mary would love to read to him also. This man was so endearing to her, and she found herself comparing him to her father, whom she adored. His commitment to his son and his community were to be respected. He had honor and integrity and a regard for humanity she found admirable. She couldn't understand why he was still single after this many years since his wife died. Aislinn was positive there had been women who had expressed their interest in a relationship with him. David was, after all, an attractive and intelligent man with family values. She couldn't help but wonder if he hadn't made some promise to his wife he felt he had to hold up in order to honor her for their son. She tried to appear busy as he entered the room so he wouldn't think she had been eavesdropping.

"I apologize once again," David explained sheepishly.

"You have no reason to apologize to me," Aislinn assured him. "Important matters always take precedence."

David took the seat next to her at the table, leaning in toward her so he could see the laptop screen with her. He could smell the perfume scent of her hair as she moved her head about beside him. Occasionally stray wafts of her hair would touch against his cheek, bringing about a sensation of tiny shock waves throughout his body, causing him to move away abruptly before she noticed how her presence affected him.

"The very first part," Aislinn began, oblivious to his discomfort at the moment. "See where it begins with 'Filleann an feall ar an bhfeallaire,' which means, 'The bad deed returns on the bad deed doer.' Apparently, this guy wronged someone who, instead of letting it go, decided to take revenge, and from the looks of it, they were pretty upset with this guy."

"There doesn't appear to be a connection between the murders other than they all knew one another," David explained, rubbing his hand through his hair. "I have reviewed recent cases, and there were none that would warrant this type of anger. There's a definite link, but I just can't figure out what it is yet, but I don't believe it has anything to do with any court cases."

"Maybe the next part will help shed more light. It says, 'Da fhada an la tagann an trathnon,'" Aislinn pronounced each word with perfection and glanced over at David to see if he was following along before proceeding with the translation. "Which means, 'No matter how long the day, the evening comes.' The final inscription on the body concludes with 'Nil luibh na leigheas in aghaidh an bhais,' translated 'There is no remedy or cure against death.' I believe each of these people have, in some manner, definitely upset the wrong people."

"The question is, who?" David surmised, asking her to translate the pictures of the pavement around Mr. Ball. "Were they members of an organization and they crossed the wrong person or persons? I don't have anything but these inscriptions, and they don't really indicate what their grief with each of the victims is. I do know they have a history of unscrupulous and questionable behaviors."

"This part is like a message to you," Aislinn explained why she felt that way before beginning the translation. "This says, 'Necessity knows no law, need teaches a plan, patience is poultice for all wounds, even a small thorn causes festering,' and then it goes on to say, 'It is sweet to drink but bitter to pay for' and concludes with 'Listen to the sound of the river and you will get a trout.' The last part strikes me as being separate from the other words. I get a gut feeling it is a message to those working the case. Whoever is committing these crimes is trying to tell you something. I may be going way out on the limb here, but that is my instinct."

"We are fully aware the two of them were close buddies and worked together for many years," David replied with a hint of aggravation. "Apparently the two of them crossed paths with the wrong people in some of their activities, but who remains the issue. I am going to have to go back to some old files and see if I can't find some sort of connection that would make sense of all this. These were definitely executions performed by a professional, but finding the link will be the trick."

"Are you saying you think they have some ties to the Irish mafia?" Aislinn asked while continuing to flip through the photos she had taken. "These were definitely executions, but what would the Irish mafia want with these small players unless, of course, they are tied to something much bigger."

"My guess is they are involved in more than this sleepy little town knows," David warned before sharing more information. "There have been several young ladies disappear from the surrounding area, and no one has seen or heard from them. Searches turn up empty, but they all had one thing in common, at least that's what each of their families reported."

"What is that?" Aislinn asked, intrigued to hear his answer.

"They were all involved with drugs and prostitution," David advised and then paused before continuing. "It doesn't explain what happened to several teens, both male and female, who just vanished with absolutely no trace. Their families all had similar stories to share about their missing children having been good kids, students, active in church with no sign of any drug activity."

"Were there any commonalities there?" she asked. Deep inside, her own mind now wondering what happened to those poor children.

"They were all talented and good-looking kids," David explained, "which leads me to think those kids have been taken so that some sick piece of shit can get their rocks off with them."

"I wish you hadn't told me that part," Aislinn whispered softly as tears streamed down each cheek of her face. "It isn't that I don't feel bad for adults who suffer atrocities, but children are so innocent and haven't even had time to figure out who they are yet. How can people be so sick and not even realize they are sick?"

"I wish I had an explanation and a cure for their madness." David spoke in a soothing tone while reaching his arm around her and drawing her closer to him. Aislinn leaned her head against his chest and shoulder and wiped at the tears with the back of her hand. "I didn't mean to upset you, Aislinn. I have asked a lot from you today, and I am sure you are overwhelmed from my expectations of you. I apologize for involving you in this case, but I truly needed your professionalism on that scene today."

"Please don't apologize," Aislinn assured as she tilted her head to look at him. "I have always dreamt of doing just this, and it is my own expectations which overwhelm me, not yours, Detective."

Aislinn's mouth sat inches away from his. David merely only need to lean forward and he could taste the moistness her lips offered up to him at this moment. He could feel his breathing become labored as he continued to look deep into those haunting green eyes as she continued to gaze up at him. He felt a stirring in his loin he thought had long been forgotten. He wanted this woman more than he had ever desired any woman, but he did not want it to be like this. No, he wanted everything to be as perfect as she was and deserved. He found it difficult to turn away from those sea green eyes that fought hard to keep his gaze, but after several minutes, he was able to slowly move away and stand before proceeding across the room away from her. Yes, he needed to put distance between them, and he would be able to think more clearly.

Aislinn was surprised by his abrupt actions and asked if everything was fine as she thought they were having a wonderful conversation.

David assured her everything was fine before explaining he had a lot of work to do at the office and asked if she could give him a ride to the station so he could pick up his Jeep. He was quiet and reserved during the ride, speaking mostly about weather and sports. Anything that would distract him from the thoughts of her that caused a reaction in him, he hadn't allowed for years. He was slightly disappointed in his own behavior and inability to control his emotions in her presence. He thought he had mastered all these matters until he met her. She was as mysterious as she was readable and intriguing and not simply for her physical beauty but for the manner in which she presented herself along with her intellect. His emotions were battling between the need to be in her presence and the need to be in more control of himself and his emotions. He thanked her as she pulled to end of the parking lot to let him off next to his Jeep. He closed the door to her car gently and strolled toward his vehicle.

"Detective Hough," she called out her window. "Thanks again for allowing me to help you. You have given me a lot to research, and I love researching."

He turned and smiled before climbing in the Jeep and turning the key to the ignition. David threw it in reverse and barked tires on his way out of the lot. He had something he needed to check out that had been eating at him ever since he and Aislinn mentioned the Irish mafia.

CHAPTER 11

O Me! O Life!

O Me! O life!…of the questions of these recurring;
Of the endless trains of the faithless—of cities fill'd with the foolish;
Of myself forever reproaching myself, (for who
more foolish than I, and who more faithless?)
Of eyes that vainly crave the light—of the objects
mean—of the struggle ever renew'd;
Of the poor results of all—of the plodding
and sordid crowds I see around me;
Of the empty and useless years of the rest—
with the rest me intertwined;
The question, O me! so sad, recurring—
What good amid these, O me, O life?
Answer.
That you are here—that life exists, and identity;
That the powerful play goes on, and you will contribute a verse.

—Walt Whitman, *Leaves of Grass*

The stranger read aloud one of her father's favorite authors and books. She loved sitting by the fireside, listening to her father read from the very book she held in her hands. She could feel the flames of the fire lick at her exposed flesh as she sat close to the hearth to warm herself. The earlier storm brought a cool front with it, making it necessary to light the fireplace since she wasn't sure how much fuel or even how safe the furnace would be after years of sitting unattended. She definitely didn't want to do anything that might draw unwanted attention from anyone who might be out wondering the woods. She supposed the cabin being in the location her father chose was part of the reason it had gone unnoticed by vagrants, hunters, and others who might be looking for mischief. It also kept the elements from causing damage to the wood frame with the winters that fell on the state of Michigan. She was impressed with her father's knowledge and skill and pleased that most of it had been passed on to her. He would have been proud of her dedication, endless hard work, and exhaustive training she endured in order to complete with no errors the plan she had worked for so long.

A smile crossed her face as she decided to leave the warmth of the fire to look for something to eat. She had packed several nonperishable items and had stopped by the grocery and a bakery to pick up a few things she could enjoy for moments such as this. The bag of marshmallows caught her eye, and she couldn't resist the temptation of s'mores floating in her head. She grabbed the box of graham crackers, bag of marshmallows, and a chocolate bar and sauntered back to the fire. Setting the items on the hearth, she adjusted the rug and blanket from off the sofa and settled in once again by the fire.

She satisfied her craving with a couple of the scrumptious treats and settled back against the pillow; retrieving the book beside her, she read another of her favorite quotes her father had marked in the book. She couldn't have agreed more with the words she read aloud:

> Not I, nor anyone else can travel that road for you.
> You must travel it by yourself.
> It is not far. It is within reach.
> Perhaps you have been on it since you were born,
> and did not know.
> Perhaps it is everywhere—on water and land."
>
> —Walt Whitman, Leaves of Grass

CHAPTER 12

David entered the doors to the station and greeted one of his coworkers as he made his way to his office. Clare staffed seven full-time officers, including the chief. It had been a quiet little town where not much happened besides your occasional domestic argument, accident, or bar fight until the recent events that took place and turned the town upside down.

Reporters from the surrounding areas made their way into town to see if they could get a scoop, and David had been good at avoiding them until he ran into Aislinn. She had managed to change some of his views regarding reporters over the past few weeks as he saw her as one of the true investigative reporters who actually do research before sensationalizing a story based on assumptions. She was brilliant and had given him a lot to think about earlier. She was willing to forgo her own story to help him with the case, which told him what he needed to know about her morals and true dedication to a cause. He was sick and tired of hearing people say, 'It's my job,' when their one and only job was to tell the truth, not half of it in order to slant it to propagate their own agenda.

David pulled up the file bank of recent drug-related arrests and searched the names for any possible link or connections with any of the Irish mafia gangs. David was particularly interested in the K&A gang out of Philadelphia since they had been heavily involved in the making of methamphetamines and prostitution. David had recalled they originated in what is referred to as the Philadelphia Badlands. It is an Irish American section of North Philadelphia, Pennsylvania, United States, that in the 1980s and '90s became known for an abundance of open-air recreational drug markets and drug-related violence. He could remember when it first made its way into their small community, creating a rise in crimes unfamiliar to this small town in its previous years. The effects the drug had on its users was astounding and didn't take any time for their physical appearances to change. Most of the users had open sores where they would dig their skin, their teeth began to rot within the first few months from the harsh chemicals in the drug, their faces appeared gaunt and lifeless, but what caught David's attention the most was the lack of life in the eyes of each of them.

One of the defendants, Mikey O'Hare, who had been arrested and linked to several assaults and possession of narcotics in Clare, caught the detective's attention, having come from Philadelphia where his arrest record was extensive. He had moved to the Detroit area after his encounters with law enforcement in Clare and was apparently murdered back in 2007 for entering someone else's turf and interfering with their business productivity and finances. The detective noted a very interesting fact that later revealed O'Hare had been related to the deceased prosecutor. He was the late prosecutor's nephew, born to his sister and brother-in-law, who resided in Pennsylvania to present. According to records, Mikey was never formally charged for any of the crimes he had committed within Clare city limits. It seems the prosecutor and the chief made an agreement with Mikey to leave town and not return or he would likely find himself behind bars.

"I'll be, she was right," David said aloud, eyes transfixed on the computer screen in front of him. "There has to be a connection." He honestly couldn't think of one person in the community who could think to murder a man the way the prosecutor and investigator were killed or smart enough to leave not even one trace of their presence. "These were, without doubt, professional hits, but why?"

David printed off the screen and picked up the receiver to his office phone and dialed one of his long-time friends whom he often bounced ideas off. They had known each other throughout school and became good friends early on. They often went on family vacations with the other since they were inseparable for the most part. It wasn't until their college careers did they take different paths due to career choices. Kevin Ballard went on to pursue his career in political science and became a senator, and David chose the quieter life with the girl of his dreams. Kevin was godfather to Gabriel and had been a good friend through the years. Kevin had been truly heartbroken for his friend when he learned of his wife's death. They would often get together on weekends and enjoy each other's company, but David withdrew after her death, explaining he didn't want to impose on Kevin and his wife, Sarah, as the odd man out. Kevin never stopped reaching out to David through his grieving, and his loyalty kept David going for his son. The two would meet a few times a year to go camping and fishing, catching up with each other and discussing recent political events. David knew Kevin would have more resources regarding the information he needed.

"David!" he heard Kevin's voice boom through the speaker. "How the hell are you, pal? It's been awhile."

"Things are good, Kevin, real good," David convinced his friend and checked to see how his family has been. "I have a favor to ask of you."

"Oh no, this is never good," Kevin teased and laughed his jovial laugh, which usually made David laugh, but not in this instance; this was a matter bigger than himself or Clare Police Department could handle, especially with their chief having taken leave without notifying any of the staff. Everyone was surprised he hadn't let anyone know he was leaving or where he was going for that matter. They figured that with the murder of the prosecutor, who was good friends with the chief, it could have possibly affected him more than they had realized. None of his children had called in to report anything suspicious, but they all lived out of town since his wife died several years earlier. They decided to give it a few days to see if he called or returned before opening an investigation for a missing person.

"Can you meet me for dinner around five at The Chop House in Grand Rapids?" David asked, knowing it was one of Keith's favorite dining places.

"You are killing me, my friend, but yes, I will see you there," Kevin replied. "Oh, why don't you bring Gabriel and he can play with the boys and maybe the two of you can spend the weekend?"

"I really wish we could do that, but I am working on this case, and I don't think I can afford the time right now." David had a sound of disappointment in his tone before telling Kevin he would see him at five and placing the receiver back in its cradle. It would take him nearly two hours to drive, so he would have to leave soon to arrive on time. He didn't like to keep people waiting as he felt being late, other than unforeseeable events occurring, was rude and disrespectful to the person left waiting.

David was disappointed he was unable to take Gabriel to spend time with Kevin's boys. He needed some extra quality time with his son since the past few weeks had kept him busy. He sat back in the seat and tried to enjoy the drive down to Grand Rapids. Normally he would have taken in the scenery from the drive he had enjoyed on previous trips, but his mind was so preoccupied with the recent murders he found it difficult to think of anything else. He had exhausted all leads on the streets and felt he had run into a dead end until Aislinn innocently flipped the switch that got his brain working at an accelerated rate he was unable to turn off.

He switched gears and came back to the prosecutor, whom he heard had been involved in some nefarious activities, but they somehow always seemed to be swept under the rug for politically motivated reasons. He knew he had missed something, but trying to figure out the link beyond their careers would be hopeless until he could speak more intimately with the families. The department had a clean record, beyond an incident involving another officer many years earlier, so there couldn't be anything linking to that case although they would have been serving during the same time but many years younger. He found it difficult to believe anyone would have waited this many years, so he dismissed the thought and turned the volume up on his stereo, and the speakers poured out the sound of a group he had grown fond of Il Divo. They were an amazing quartet whose voices blended so perfectly you could feel the hairs on your body stand up and leave your senses begging for more. The lyrics to one of their songs, "Mama," would bring David to near tears as they belted out the melody, and his thoughts went to his own mother. She had been a strong presence throughout his life, and she kept him strong after his wife died. It seemed she was gifted in consoling those who were broken, but David was never certain what her great loss was which brought so much compassion from her. She would dismiss it and laugh so as not to remember whatever it was that made his mother so loving. He couldn't recall having ever heard her say a negative word about another person, and she wasn't the type to get hysterical over matters. She confronted things with a brave heart and a smile that never seemed to disappear from her face. He admired these qualities in her and knew that when he found his own wife, he had found a younger version of his mother. He lost himself in his own thought, and it wasn't until he noticed the sign for him to get on 131S exit heading into Grand Rapids did he realize the CD had played through and had already begun repeating the songs.

David turned the volume down and switched it back to the radio and watched for his exit ramp, which would take him downtown. He always enjoyed the festivities around the annual Art Prize and was surprised by the friendliness that seemed to exude from the residents and visitors to the area. He noticed it was definitely a growing community, and the innovation used to maintain their history, but embracing new ideas, David found refreshing.

David couldn't believe he was fortunate enough to find a parking spot close to the restaurant with all the art goers. He would love to have attended the event himself this year, but it seemed that wouldn't be the case as he had been busy trying to solve the murders and be a dad at the same time. He enjoyed the different styles presented by all the artists from different corners of the earth, who came to represent their work. He was impressed by the amount of talent each artist had been gifted with. One of the many things he missed about his wife was her passion for the arts. She had broadened his horizons when it came to the arts as he had not known his own appreciation until his wife's passion also became his. He struggled entering her studio to this day as the portrait of their family was the last painting they had been working on together, and it now sits unfinished to date.

"Maybe someday," he whispered to himself as he crossed the street and made his way into the restaurant, checking around to see if Kevin had already arrived.

"Good evening, sir," the waiter greeted. "Do you have a reservation for this evening with us?"

"Yes, I do," David replied cordially. "It is under Hough. I am awaiting the senator, so if you would like to advise him where the table is on his arrival, that would be great."

"Gladly, sir. Just follow me this way and I will provide you with a private dining area so you won't be disturbed," the waiter replied, gathering two menus, napkins, and silverware for the table before leading David to a table near the end of the restaurant where it appeared to be much more intimate for the privacy of their conversation.

David's sense of smell took in the rich aromas of the steak wafting in the air around him, along with the sides that came with the different choices. The waiter poured him a glass of water and asked if he would like to start with a drink while he waited.

"The water will be fine for now, thank you," David advised while taking the opportunity to browse through the menu while he waited for Kevin.

"As you wish, sir. I will check on you periodically to see if I can be of assistance." And with that the waiter excused himself and went about other duties while David continued to look at the many splendid dishes offered. Halfway through the menu choices, he glanced up and saw his old friend approaching the table accompanied by the same waiter who had seated him.

"David, it is so good to see you," Kevin informed him as he reached around David to give him a hug.

David returned the gesture, and they stood for several minutes chatting before taking their seats as the waiter stood by patiently, waiting to take their drink order.

Both agreed to an Argentinian Malbec as they had enjoyed it before it had become the rave among Americans. It had previously been difficult to order a glass in most establishments but had fast become a favorite of most patrons.

They decided to have the chilled oysters on the half shell as an appetizer while they perused the menu to determine their entrées. It was a difficult decision since the menu carried so many entrées that appealed to both of them, but David decided on steak au poivre with a salad, soup, and side of grilled asparagus with parmesan. Kevin decided to order the Australian rib lamb chops with a side of sautéed spinach with garlic. They both concluded it didn't matter what dish you ordered; they were all masterfully put together, and any would have sufficed and satisfied.

"So tell me more about what is going on," Kevin requested as the waiter left to place their orders. "It sounds like there is more to this, and it could be risky for you to take on alone. Jesus, David, these are high-profile people being murdered. Someone is very pissed off about something, and I would say it is much bigger than Clare."

"I am getting that feeling, my friend," David agreed, taking a sip of wine from the glass. "I have done some research, and I think I might be on to something. I just want to run it by you to see if it makes any sense to you."

David explained to Kevin the occurrences and advised that he had gone through all recent cases for the past five years or so and came up with nothing that would explain the link between the victims and how they were murdered. He told Kevin they were undoubtedly executions, but why was the question he was unable to answer. He shared with him the information he had obtained from the database regarding the prosecutor's nephew and his connection with the K&A gang. Kevin's face paled at the mention of the gang as he was all too familiar with some of their activities, along with a few other gangs of heavily Irish descent.

"David, I don't want you proceeding any further until I can provide you with some help and resources," Kevin warned. "It sounds that this is much bigger than your forces can handle in Clare."

"That's why I am here, Kevin," David admitted while passing off a piece of paper to the senator. "I need you to check on these matters for me, if you have an opportunity. I think there is a connection here, but I can't venture out of my district to check them out. I thought you might be able to get more information in your position than they would willingly provide to me."

Kevin made a few calls from the table with requests to check into the information David provided and advised them to get on it immediately and get back with him as soon as they found anything.

David knew he could depend on his friend and felt he had made the right move in contacting Kevin. It was a sad reminder that he had neglected to spend time with his friend as they had before the accident and decided to enjoy the remainder of their evening talking about old times and enjoying their meal together. The hours passed too quickly, and David still had the commute back to Clare, so he told Kevin he would have to leave soon.

"Promise me you will wait to hear from me before you go getting in over your head," Kevin warned again. "Gabriel needs you and so do your parents. I'd be lying if I didn't include myself in the equation."

David stood to embrace his friend once again. He reached for his wallet to pay the bill, and Kevin told him dinner was on him.

"We will be expecting you and Gabriel soon," Kevin teased. "You know how my wife is when she wants something, so consider yourself warned, my friend."

David pretended to shake in fear as he walked toward the exit, pausing for a moment to bid his friend farewell again before proceeding out the door. He strolled casually to his car and took in some of the art that was on display in the windows and on the streets as he walked.

CHAPTER 13

The following morning, Detective Hough sat hunched over his desk, staring blankly at the monitor screen of his desktop computer. He had a nervous habit of running his hands through his hair as he did now while struggling to find any logic behind the recent murders. He had dark circles around his eyes, and beneath each of them was a noticeable bag, indicative that he'd had very little sleep over the course of the past few days.

"What is the common link here?" he asked himself out loud before a knock on his office door interrupted his thoughts. "What can I do for you?"

"This package just came for you in the mail. I brought it right over," one of the desk staff advised from the other side of the door.

"Thank you, Pam," he said with a note of appreciation in his voice, turning to retrieve the package she held out to him.

"No problem," she replied, placing the package in his hand. "It looks like you could use some coffee. Not just a cup but an entire pot. Would you like for me to bring you a cup?"

"That won't be necessary, but thanks anyway," David replied, holding in his other hand his thermos half full of the steaming brew. He excused her and sat the package to the side of his desk away from the stacks of files currently littering the majority and went back to his research. He sat there for several more hours leafing through old case files, searching for any clue which might link each of the victims in some fashion other than their careers.

"Nothing!" he nearly yelled. "There is nothing, and I have gone back through ten years of files. There's a connection, and I will find it."

David had ignored the constant reminder his stomach gave him that he hadn't fed it all day until the hunger pains became a distraction. He scooted his chair from the desk and decided to pull himself from it. He bent and stretched his tired body before proceeding out of his office in search of a source of nourishment. He made his way through the halls and out the door and immediately peeled his jacket off from the heat off the sun's rays blasting down on the pavement beneath his feet. It had been cool this morning when he headed into the office, but this was late summer in Michigan. You can go from turning the heater on to needing air-conditioning within a few hours passing. He actually preferred these types of days because he was able to get a lot of physical chores finished in the cool air of the morning, and on weekends, he could enjoy the rest of the day swimming, fishing, and boating with Gabriel. It was great for camping as well. They would sit by the campfire, and David would tell stories while they roasted marshmallows over the open flame.

David hoped to give his son the memories he had as a boy growing up with his father. They spent quality time together on projects and outings and had many father-son talks regarding life and politics. David remembered being worried his father would be disappointed when he chose not to become a doctor or lawyer, but instead, he recalled how his father encouraged him to follow his heart, explaining that's where true happiness lies. David wanted to be the example for his son that his father was to him. He also learned how to treat a lady by the manner he observed in his father. He had never heard either of his parents speak an unkind word to the other, nor did he ever hear them raise their voices in anything other than laughter and cheers. His father consistently reminded him that each time you lose control of your emotions or behaviors, you lose a piece of your self-respect and set yourself back. David didn't understand this as a frustrated teen dealing with injustices by peers and typical hormonal changes, but the more he applied his father's advice, the more it revealed itself to be true. He warned that people can take anything from you, but they cannot take your beliefs or your morals. They cannot force you to be anything other than what you choose to be.

David had a clear understanding how some people become broken and then fall into the trap of losing their self-worth. He had seen it in so many of the people he'd had to arrest and charge with crimes he knew were a result of their unhealed pain. They are lost souls who were abused or neglected in ways the fortunate know nothing about. They are looked down upon by other members of society who didn't once lift a hand to reach out with a word of comfort or a warm embrace. These people have an unmet need, which plummets them into a vicious cycle of self-abuse until someone is brave enough or caring enough to hand them the rope and tools to pull themselves out of their self-destructive ways. He had, on occasion, seen his fellow officers treating some of the inmates disrespectfully, and it made his skin crawl as he reminded them they were here to rehabilitate, not punish, as these people have been tormented in their lives already or have a mental illness going untreated. He knew most of his wisdom gained from his father fell on deaf ears. His father warned him that there will be people who have no ability to empathize with anyone besides themselves, so they will never be able to relate to the needs of those who suffer to the point of self-destruction.

He recalled on many occasions when he had to hold his temper as a couple of his fellow officers took pleasure in what David considered to be cruel and unusual punishment as inmates are already stripped of their freedom, given a pad, sheet, and wool blanket to sleep on the concrete floor with a commode next to their head, forced to drink from a sink directly above the commode, which disgusted him to no avail. These morons took pleasure in degrading them further by addressing them by their last names, turning the heat up, and then turning it down to blow extremely cold air. During hourly checks, they would allow the heavy metal door to the pod area to slam loudly, disturbing any rest they could get from the lights that glared in their eyes the entire night. The only relief they could get was to cover their faces with the wool blanket provided, which meant they had to draw in a fetal position to cover their entire body. David often questioned who the actual criminals were—those who commit crimes to feed their habits of continued abuse or those who are in a position to show compassion—but instead they choose to inflict more pain to dehumanize them further. Their haughty egotistical beliefs that these people deserve this form of punishment reflect the darkness of their own souls. Had they not been so proud and self-righteous, they may have had the opportunity to make an impact on the lives whom so desperately cling to what little faith remains in them, reflected by their decision to not end their own lives, although the abuse they do to themselves would make one believe otherwise.

Aislinn immediately came to his mind as he recalled her ability where she had to capture an image and, without a word, have them speak multitude. David didn't possess the finesse she presented herself with, but he was working on himself so that he could find another means of expressing his views that could be accepted by others. He had filed complaints against some of them, but they were quickly dismissed by the chief, who told him they were under a lot of stress themselves and he should have more empathy for his fellow officers instead of lawbreakers.

He could have transferred out, but he had built his life here, and that would mean he would have to leave behind the memories he had built with his wife, and he wasn't ready to make that decision yet.

David recalled the words his father spoke as he was learning to choose his friends in life: "The most dangerous people are those who have no empathy or compassion. I would prefer to walk among thieves, liars, and beggars as I know what to expect from them, but a hypocrite is deceiving. They often come in the guise of doing good and their evil is often of a wicked and self-serving nature."

David was able to recognize people for the work they did without bringing recognition to themselves for their own glorification or motives, but they, instead, genuinely cared for those they helped. These were the people he would go out of his way to help when they were in need and did what he could to make sure they received recognition for their kindness since they didn't seek their own recognition.

With that thought in mind, David decided to have a midday lunch at the Whitehouse Restaurant, named for its appearance. It's a small establishment where all the staff are quite friendly and personable, and he needed to see smiles. He took a seat close to the window so he could look out at the sunshine in hopes of lifting his spirit.

"Good afternoon, Detective," the waiter addressed him in a cheerful tone. "What can I get for you today?"

"I will have my usual, Betty," David replied, which meant he would have the Greek burger, one of the restaurant's specialties. It's a double lamb burger with melted feta, lettuce, tomato, and onions on a fresh brioche bun with a side of tzatziki.

"Water with that or do you need coffee today?" she asked, a concerned look on her face.

"I believe I will stick with the water today," he replied, smiling because he understood her question. "Thanks anyway."

David turned back to the window and allowed himself to take in the beauty of the day briefly before turning his thoughts back to his work, with the occasional distraction of visions of Aislinn. There was so much he thought he knew about her but so much that remained a mystery to him. He felt he had to know more as she had drawn him to her like a moth to a flame.

CHAPTER 14

Aislinn spent most of the day sitting in front of her laptop, researching potential correlations between the messages left by the murderer and the victims. She checked all sites pertaining to the goddess Morrigan to see if there had been something she had missed or misinterpreted, but she couldn't find anything disputing her original knowledge of the tale. She couldn't help but believe that if she could be granted permission to review some of the files, she could help the detective in his research. She thought it couldn't hurt to ask, so she placed a call to David's office and left him a message on his office phone to return her call at his convenience.

Feeling she had done all she could at the moment, she decided she would visit a few places in town and talk to some of the locals to see if they would be willing to give their views on the situation happening in their community.

Instead of driving, she decided to take a leisurely stroll on her bike and rode about the streets of Clare, enjoying the sunshine and beautiful weather. She would greet people who were running about the town on their errands and lunch breaks and would approach those who appeared to not be in a hurry. She noted that not one person she had approached yet appeared willing to discuss the matter openly, and their uneasiness was evident. She sensed an air of fear over the town that went deeper than the recent murders. One had gone so far as to tell her that she will leave town soon, but they have nowhere else to go. When she asked what they meant by their statement, she was met with a blank stare and silence. She knew there was certainly more to the situation than the townspeople were willing to share, and this only increased her desire to dig deeper into the history of the town and its matters.

Turning her bike toward E. Fourth Street, she decided to take a visit to Pere Marquette District Library to check through their artifacts and history on the city. *Old newspaper archives may hold something worth knowing*, she thought. She spoke with the librarian to explain she wasn't a resident and wasn't sure what she would need to do to access records in their library unless she could be provided a temporary card. The librarian was helpful and was happy to show Aislinn where to look for records pertaining to the community. Aislinn took notes on anything she thought might be helpful, and when she came across several records on file regarding missing persons, her interest was immediately piqued. She jotted down some of the names of the families who had sent out pleas, begging for the return of their child. *This may be the break I needed*, she told herself.

Gathering her notebook, she thanked the librarian once again and exited the building to see if she could find a telephone book which might give her an idea of the whereabouts of the families so that she could visit them to see if they would be willing to share their stories with her. With public phone booths being almost non-existent today, she was having difficulty locating one, so she decided to visit a local establishment and asked if she could use theirs. She explained she wasn't from the area and needed to get some addresses, and they were happy to oblige. She flipped through the pages for the names on her list and was able to locate some she felt might be the same people. She jotted down the addresses to the ones she could locate and decided to return to the cottage for her car. She wasn't sure how far some of them were from town, and she felt she could get to each quicker by driving. She made her way back through the streets toward the cottage, pedaling as fast as her legs would allow her, hoping she would be able to speak to most of the list she had copied. She couldn't understand how this many disappearances didn't warrant a special investigation by the FBI, especially since no bodies of the missing were ever found. None of it made any sense to her, and she felt there was much more than obviously the townspeople knew either.

Aislinn pushed the bicycle onto the back porch and locked the door before climbing in her car and heading to the closest address. She had mapped them out in the area so she could travel from one to the next without wasting too much driving time between each stop. She pulled in front of the first house and walked to the door. It was apparent to her that someone was home because they had the main door open to allow the breeze to blow through the screened door. Unable to locate a doorbell, she knocked gently on the screen door and waited for a response. After a few minutes without a response, she knocked harder and heard a female voice from inside tell her to hold on a minute. Aislinn stepped back from the door and waited for the face that went with the voice to appear.

"What can I do for you?" a lady who appeared to be in her mid-forties asked from the other side of the screen.

Aislinn took in her appearance and noted the woman had a tired look to her, as if she wasn't receiving the proper amount of rest. Aislinn wasn't judging, but she noticed the woman was clean but didn't make any effort toward her appearance beyond showering.

"Hi, ma'am, are you Mrs. Beecher?" Aislinn inquired.

"I am," she replied, remaining behind the screen door. "What do you need?"

"I am sorry to disturb your day," Aislinn began. "But I was wondering if I might have a few minutes of your time to talk to you about your daughter Christie."

"What about my daughter?" She nearly flew to the door and was standing in front of Aislinn, her eyes wide with what appeared to be fear.

Aislinn quickly explained who she was and why she came to talk with her about the disappearance of her daughter. Mrs. Beecher seemed to relax a little the more Aislinn explained, but this was a woman who had been living for years, waiting for news of her daughter. The suffering she lived showed on her physical body and her emotional well-being. Aislinn could only imagine the pain this woman dealt with every day she opened her eyes due to the unknowing. Was her daughter alive or dead was a question she asked herself daily. Mrs. Beecher invited Aislinn inside so they could sit and talk about what she knew or had been told by those in authority. Listening to the woman talk about her daughter, it was obvious there was foul play involved with her disappearance. Mrs. Beecher showed her Christie's room, which hadn't been touched since the day of her disappearance besides the occasional dusting. She had kept it like a memorial of her daughter and hope that she would one day return to her. Christie was involved in sports and had been on the honor society. The photos she had of her and her friends showed a happy teen who didn't appear to have any drug-related problems, and from listening to her mother, she was a wonderful young lady with a bright future.

Each family Aislinn visited after leaving Mrs. Beecher all had the same look of sadness in their eyes. Some worked harder to cover up their loss and grief, but Aislinn could see the heaviness of their loss in their faces and eyes. It seemed that most of the families she spoke with had no indication their child was struggling with any type of addiction or a need to run away. They mostly came from middle-class families where both parents worked, but the kids themselves never presented problems in the home or the school environment. They were all attractive in their physical appearance, which led Aislinn to believe there was something very evil that had taken place in this town over the years, and she wanted to help solve the disappearances to provide each of the families with an idea of what happened to their loved ones. She knew there was something much bigger going on, and she felt the recent murders might possibly be a clue to discovering what happened to them. *Could there be a possible connection between all the happenings?* she asked herself. There were too many unanswered questions and things which simply didn't make any sense to her.

When she finished at the last home for the day, she checked her phone to see if the detective had returned her call. When she saw he hadn't, she decided to stop by the station to see if she could catch him in his office.

Arriving at the station, she could see his Jeep sitting in the back of the lot and decided to walk in to see if he was in his office. She was greeted by the desk officer, who told her to take a seat and he would page the detective for her.

Aislinn took the seat closest to the window and watched the officer dial David's extension and was relieved when she heard him tell him he had a visitor and gave her name. Moments later, the heavy locked door opened and David stood holding it open and called to her. She gathered her things and followed him through the door and down the hall to his office. He closed the door behind him and told her to take a seat. She looked around his space and saw several photos of him and Gabriel, along with several drawings and paintings Gabriel had made for him that David had framed and hung in the office. She noticed the stacks of files everywhere on his desk and the undeniable fatigue present on his face.

"I am sorry to interrupt your work, but I have been checking out some things today I thought you might find of interest," she explained, and not waiting for his approval, she continued to tell him about speaking with some of the families of the children who have been missing over the years.

"Aislinn, what are you doing?" David asked with an air of impatience. "Why would you get these families all worked up again?"

"That wasn't my intention, David," she replied in a similar tone. "I believe there is a connection between the missing kids and the recent murders."

"I am sorry," he apologized. "I am just overwhelmed with this mess, and I don't need the families burning up my phone and creating a distraction in this investigation."

"I don't think you have to worry about that," she continued to explain. "I told them who I was, and my purpose was to see how far each of the investigations had gone. David, none of the disappearances make any sense. These kids were good students and had no history of any problems in their families or school."

"What makes you think they are related to the murders?" he asked in a much friendlier tone this time.

"Do you remember when we talked about the K&A gang?" she asked. "They are affiliated with sex slavery, and each of these kids had attractive features and talent. They would make their abductors plenty of money with the right johns. I just have a bad feeling about this. It just doesn't seem right."

David leaned back in his chair and ran his hands through his hair, pondering over what she had just told him. He was even more impressed with her investigative skills, but her fearlessness frightened him for her sake.

"Okay, let's say there is some connection," he began explaining. "If that's the case, then whoever is responsible could possibly still be here and you just stepped on their toes. Aislinn, I can't have you going all over town running your own investigation without checking with me first. You could be setting yourself up for something very bad, and I can't allow you to do that."

"I don't see how talking to families about their missing children could possibly put me in any danger," she argued, somewhat perturbed he was under the impression she couldn't take care of herself.

"If there is any connection, as you are suggesting, then how can it not put you in danger?" he asked, seeming to lose his patience with her bravado. "Look around you, Aislinn. People are missing and dead. What more do I need to say?"

"I am sorry that I wasted your time, Detective," Aislinn stated as she stood from the chair and started to make her way toward the door. "I know you have a lot on your mind, and I won't disturb you again."

"Hold on a minute," David suggested, standing himself to try to convince her to remain. "That's not what I was suggesting, Aislinn, and I do respect and appreciate your work. You have been an asset to my investigation. My point is, I don't want to investigate another scene and discover you are the victim. I am simply asking that you please keep me informed of your findings and check with me before you do anything like this in the future, please."

Feeling sorry for him now, she let her guard down and thanked him for being concerned for her well-being before reminding him of her ninja skills, which brought laughter to both of them for the moment. They were able to communicate more openly again, and to make up for being short with her, David asked if she would join him for dinner later at his house. He explained he would have invited her out to a restaurant, but Mary had already planned dinner and was expecting him.

Aislinn immediately agreed as it would give her another opportunity to visit with Mary and Gabriel.

"Shall I pick you up on my way from the office?" David asked, smiling that crooked grin that seemed to stop her heart periodically. "If you prefer to drive yourself, I can come by so that you can follow me."

"No, it will be fine for you to pick me up unless you prefer to remain home once you are there," she replied, turning to walk toward the door, and in doing so, her purse nearly knocked to the floor an envelope sitting at the edge of his desk. She caught it before it fell to the floor, and as she went to place it back on the desk, David told her to go ahead and hand it to him as he had forgotten he had set it there. Obligingly, he handed it to him and told him she would see him soon and departed through the door. "I can find my way out, Detective."

David stood in the doorway and watched as she made her way toward the exit to the lobby before taking the seat once again behind his desk. He had forgotten he had placed the envelope there from earlier today, so he took out his envelope opener and cracked open the seal of the envelope. David sat in awe of the contents of the envelope. It was a letter to him from the murderer, implying with proof evidence everything Aislinn had indicated to him moments earlier.

"How could she have known?" he asked himself, still looking at the letter in stunned amazement. "How did I not see the connection myself?"

David carefully placed the contents back into the envelope which it came without touching it any more than he had already. He hoped any remaining evidence hadn't been destroyed by everyone who had already come in contact with it and handled it.

David sprinted down the hall to Pam's office, hoping she hadn't left for the day. He was thankful to see her still sitting at her desk and asked her if the package had been delivered by a postman or a person when it arrived. His hopes were high they delivered it themselves and the station security cameras would have picked them up, but his dream was quickly dashed when she told him it had been delivered with several other packages by Prestige.

David ignored the quizzical look on his face and turned to leave her office with no explanation why he had inquired. He knew without a doubt he was going to need assistance from an outside source. Kevin was his only hope since David didn't know who he could trust within the local system. He made his way back to his office and placed the envelope in a large plastic bag to prevent further damaging any evidence that may remain. He grabbed his jacket from the coatrack behind the door and made his way out of the building and to his Jeep before dialing his friend. After several rings, it went to Kevin's voice mail, and David left a lengthy message for his friend, hoping he would return the call soon. David exited the parking lot at the station and drove in the direction of one of the places indicated in the letter to him, in the meanwhile trying to understand why the murderer would help him when they could clearly be implicated themselves.

When he knew he was nearing the place, he found a pull-off where he could park his car without it being detected, and he would walk the distance through the woods until he was able to get a clear view of the location. David cocked his gun in case he needed to be ready for a setup and placed another under his pants' right leg. After all, he thought if this were truly the killer, why would they want to help him? They had already murdered two people, so he knew they would have no problem killing him. He made his way through the new thicket on the floor of the forest and crept quietly when he felt he was close to the location. He saw movement in his left peripheral and quietly lowered himself to the ground behind a felled tree and watched as two men exited an out building and walked in the direction of a house. David wasn't able to recognize either of them as anyone he knew from town, and from the chemical smell in the air, he knew the killer hadn't deceived him. This was definitely a meth lab, and from the size of the outbuilding, he could bet they were a decent-sized operation. David worked his way quietly back to where he had left his car, and once he returned, he checked the time and realized he would have to wait to look into the other information until the following day. He had to pick Aislinn up, and he had more questions for her than she had probably asked in her entire career as an investigative reporter.

He ran different scenarios over and over in his mind during the drive to pick her up. He needed a way to find out how she figured it out without giving away the letter to her. The only person who knew of that evidence was Kevin, and he still hadn't heard from him, but he knew his friend could be tied up in a meeting and would call him as soon as he listened to the message. His biggest challenge at the moment was figuring out how Aislinn made the connection. He thought it clearly made sense to him now with the information the killer provided, but how did Aislinn put it together without it? he questioned. This would undoubtedly be an interesting evening, but he hadn't been disappointed with her company yet. She definitely had her alluring qualities, and he had allowed her to elude his questions before, but tonight he would not be as gracious. He needed to know, and she would have no other choice than to share with him her knowledge.

He pulled in the drive near the cottage and walked the path to her front door and rang the old-style doorbell that required the visitor to turn it rather than press it. He was taken aback when she opened the door wearing a lovely red dress and her hair in an updo that defined the physical beauty of her perfect features. He stood momentarily staring before offering his arm to her to walk her to the Jeep. David opened the door and waited for her to situate herself before closing the door. He wanted to kick himself for acting like a teenager on his first date, but he knew she would notice the gesture.

"You look absolutely stunning this evening," he assured her after adjusting himself behind the steering wheel of the car. "Red is a fitting color for you."

"Thank you," she replied, clearly able to detect his discomfort. "I recall my father telling me that once when I was younger."

"Are your parents still living?" David asked, beginning his questioning.

"Yes," she replied. "They live over near Wolverine in the same house I grew up in as a child."

"Do you have any siblings?" he continued, making it appear he was making small talk.

"No, I am an only child," Aislinn shared. "I suppose maybe once I was born they found me to be too much of a handful and decided one child was enough for them."

David looked at her in disbelief and, after seeing the smile on her face, concluded she was teasing him. Determined to stay the course, he asked her several more questions about her youth and where she attended college.

Aislinn didn't appear to suspect his questioning and cheerfully shared some of her experiences growing up. She explained that she had been homeschooled by her parents, so her friends were mostly children of her parents' friends or neighborhood kids. She hadn't experienced events, such as prom and homecoming dances, but some of her stories reflected she had received a very thorough education and could be a factor in her ability to recognize circumstances which weren't as obvious to others.

David had to credit himself with not having firsthand knowledge of many of the events which occurred in Clare prior to his relocating to the area, beyond old files he was given to review. He had heard some of the local gossip, but he preferred to be successful in establishing several programs in the city, which were youth oriented. He felt that it may have been due to his having a son and wanting positive programs that lifted and encouraged youth to discover those things they enjoyed and were naturally talented at. David wanted to provide funding for families whose children wouldn't otherwise receive lessons in art, music, dance, writing, and other activities and sports of their interest. He wanted each child to be the individual they were and to be accepted and appreciated for their uniqueness. Granted Clare wasn't able to provide every child lessons in some areas of interest due to its small population and resources available. This is why David wanted to fund opportunities in order for a family to travel or have transportation provided for their child to get what they need from a much larger city near them. He would visit the school, and the majority of the kids knew him because of his close involvement in their lives. It was easy for him to recognize the kids who were most at risk and would give them extra attention. He was familiar with some of the families of the kids he worked closely with. David was able to empathize with their needs because he knew, one day, his own son would feel the loss of his mother on days others aren't aware of and hoped they would offer compassion instead of ridicule.

"What made you feel these missing kids were linked to these recent murders?" David came right out and asked.

"Honestly, I had no clue until I went to the library yesterday and pulled archived articles," she began her explanation. "We had already talked about the gang activity, and with so many kids missing in the surrounding areas, I felt they had to be connected. These kids came from caring families and had bright futures. None of it made sense until I considered what the gang is known for, and it all seemed so clear. They have been taking these kids and putting them in the sex slave trade. That's the only thing that could possibly explain why not even one body has been located out of all of them."

"That does make logical sense," David agreed, feeling guilty inside for having doubted she would have a reasonable explanation for her knowledge. "The chief assigned the missing kids' cases to Grady, and I was warned not to interfere with his investigation when I first arrived in town, so I focused more on creating programs for the kids since not much really happens that requires my hidden detective skills."

"I honestly believe that had you been assigned, these kids would already be back with their parents, safe and reconstructing their lives," Aislinn assured him of her belief in him. "There is more to this entire madness than you or I will probably ever know, but I have a feeling those kids are still out there and are waiting for someone to find them."

David felt the murderer was trying to tell him where he could find them, but why? Was she somehow involved with the prosecutor and investigator? He had so many unanswered questions going through his mind. He knew he needed to take a break so that he could clear his mind and allow himself to rest if he was to answer any of his own questions. He knew with certainty the killer was telling the truth, and he also knew he was going to need an outside team to help him in taking down the meth labs and sex slave ring.

"How about we agree to put all this aside for the evening and enjoy this fine meal Mary has waiting for us?" David insisted as they pulled into the drive to his cabin.

"I can agree to that." Aislinn sighed with relief. "It has been quite taxing."

She followed David into the house where she could smell the aroma of their dinner wafting throughout the space. She could hear Mary and Gabriel in the kitchen in excited laughter as he helped her roll out the piecrust for her lemon meringue pie. He had more flour on his face than the counter and made an adorable sight to see.

"Whoa!" David exaggerated before going behind Gabriel and lifting him in the air. "It smells amazing in here, you two."

"Hi, Aislinn!" Gabriel squealed in excitement. "I am happy you joined us."

David feigned injury that Gabriel hadn't acknowledged him, and Gabriel laughed and told him he was being silly because he tells him every day. David placed him back on the floor to finish the pie dough while excusing himself to take the call he had coming in.

Aislinn asked if there was anything she could do to be of help, and Mary told her to just have a seat and enjoy herself. She offered Aislinn a drink of her choice, and she opted for water for the time being. She was enjoying watching Gabriel learn how to cook and having fun in his learning experience. It was obvious to her that Mary received just as much joy in teaching Gabriel and watching him grow into such a fine young man as she was enjoying watching them together.

Mary had planned a very special meal when she heard from David that Aislinn would be joining them this evening. She really liked the young woman when she met her. She got a good feeling from her, and Mary was astute at knowing people. She had a feeling Aislinn may have experienced some traumatic pain in her life, which led her to be the kind and thoughtful young lady she is, or she had parents who actually spent time teaching her kindness. Either way,

Mary had determined she was a wonderful person and hoped to see more of her.

After helping Gabriel put the crust in the piedish, she asked him to get himself cleaned up and ready for dinner.

Aislinn asked if she could at least help with setting the table, which appeared Mary had already been working on with candles and placemats for a setting of four. She aligned the silverware for each setting and placed a napkin in each drinking glass before asking if there was anything else she could help with.

Mary called out to David and Gabriel to join them for their dinner as it was ready to be served. Gabriel came out and had cleaned himself up nicely from the traces of flour that speckled his face earlier. David opened the door to his bedroom where he had taken his call and the opportunity to change his clothes into something much more relaxed to the dismay of Mary who looked at him with disapproval.

"What, Mary?" David asked in a hushed tone, looking down at his jeans and sweater.

"You know what?" she whispered while turning her eyes toward Aislinn who had clearly dressed for the evening. "It's too late to change now because dinner is ready, but think about it, David. She took the time to clean up for you."

David felt like a scorned child on his way to join the others at the table, but when Mary served him his plate, he knew she had forgiven him for his choice of attire.

She had made one of her special Irish dishes of balsamic pecan pork chops, which were rosemary-marinated pork chops, drizzled with a balsamic cider glaze, caramelized blue cheese, and candied pecans. She served these with homemade rolls, mashed potatoes, and asparagus. She had been thinking of Aislinn when she made her choice for dinner and hoped she would find it pleasing, but David was enjoying it all the same.

They laughed and talked over dinner while enjoying the fine cooking skills Mary displayed with the meal and dessert she had prepared for them.

Aislinn had enjoyed a few glasses of wine over the course of the meal and evening conversation, but David limited his to one glass since he would be driving her back to her cottage. He had lost his wife from a drunk driver crossing the lines and hitting her head-on, and he never wanted to be that person responsible for such a huge loss in another's life. He sipped at his glass of water and enjoyed the laughter of the evening, forgetting briefly of the horrors occurring in the outside world right there in his small community. He didn't want the evening to end, but the time was getting late, and he needed to drive to Grand Rapids again to meet with Kevin and share what had been sent him in hopes of discovering who was committing the murders. Kevin had offered to allow David to help pick his team from the candidates he had in mind, and they already knew they would have to penetrate the town slowly so as not to bring awareness of their presence before they could locate all the places provided in the list he had received. He questioned how safe Aislinn was now that she had managed to contact several of the families.

"Aislinn, I need you to promise me that you won't do more investigating on your own," he pleaded, hoping she would not make him go into any great detail as to why he was so worried.

"I won't speak with any of the other families so as not to cause you any further grief," she agreed. "I can't sit idly by doing nothing though, David. I am an investigator, and that's what we do. We seek the truth in order to inform people properly."

"Will you at least check with me before you speak with anyone else regarding any of the missing or murdered?" he asked, hoping she would agree once more.

"If I feel there is a reason to let you know, I will," she concluded, but providing him no commitment.

"That wasn't very reassuring," he surmised, realizing she didn't agree with his request.

"It's the best I can provide you." She smiled and stepped out of the car without waiting for him to make it around the car to open her door. He ran a couple of steps to catch up with her as she made her way down the path. "Thank you for a wonderful evening, and the dinner was magnificent as well. Mary is most amazing."

"That she is." David smiled, rubbing his belly in agreement, before turning back toward the path, unaware Aislinn watched him from the other side of the curtain.

David drove the distance back home in silence. He had turned the radio off, and his thoughts went back to why the killer would help him when they so obviously had a deep hatred for the judicial system and law. He desperately wanted to get inside the head of the person responsible for consuming hours of lost sleep and discover what had gone so wrong in their life they would resort to actual murder.

CHAPTER 15

"Only one left." The stranger sat back against the sofa, studying what appeared to be a map of surrounding area. She had used different color codes to locate the places she had discovered producing meth and running child sex slavery. She hadn't failed to take photos of the johns and wrote down their plate numbers for easy identification. The identities of them sickened her as they were people in positions most would never consider performing such sickening acts. "I am afraid you will finally be exposed, you sick bastards. I would like nothing more than to kill you myself, but then I am only here to take care of my personal business. You are merely a casualty of my war. Let their families deal with their tragedies since they didn't seem to care about mine. People nowadays seem to only feel pain when it directly involves their own loss. Then and only then can they even relate to another's pain. Most of humanity is pathetic and self-centered!"

She continued to put together pieces for the detective to be certain there were no mistakes or any of those involved missed in error. She wanted a clean sweep of the entire area so that the people in the community could move forward in a new direction conducive to their families and their future well-being.

"You, bastards, did one favor for me," she spouted through gritted teeth. "I don't have to worry about bringing another person into this world as you took care of that on that night."

She sat back and pondered briefly what her life would have been like had they not murdered her family and destroyed everything she had ever known. She wondered if she would already be married and raising children of her own, but that was not to be, she told herself, as fate rode in like a dark cloud that fretful night, sealing out the light and air, leaving behind a sickening smell, nauseating and blinding her to any hope of future happiness. She refused to hope for anything good as she never wanted to feel that type of loss again in her life. Putting aside her thoughts, she continued perfecting the map to preciseness, leaving no room for error. Satisfied she hadn't missed any of the details, she placed it inside the envelope addressed to Detective Hough and sat it to the side of the table to mail later.

Her thoughts went to the family who had taken her in and how they had tried so hard to help her to overcome the tragedy in her life. Her father had been correct in choosing them because they had managed to keep her alive when she so desperately wanted nothing more than to die and join her family. They continued to talk to her although she refused to speak one word for the first few months she was in their care. She would lie in her bed in their home, and they would visit her often, bringing her food and personally feeding her since she refused to come down for dinner. They read to her daily and shared their day with her. They were a lovely older couple who had never had children, so they devoted much of their time to helping others and enjoying nature. Bob and Doris were fine people, and she had fond feelings for them both.

Bob was a member of the Michigan Militia in the Wolverine area and happily took the responsibility when his friend contacted him, telling him the child couldn't remain in the Clare area. The person her father had told her to contact was able to retrieve her immediately, but she couldn't remember who he was or even recall what he looked like. He had her medically treated by a close friend who knew the dangers in her identity being discovered if he took her to the hospital. She awoke in the home of Bob and Doris and had forgotten briefly who she was. They had coddled and rocked her when she awoke screaming as the memories played out in her dreams and allowed her to sob endlessly in their arms. The young girl enjoyed journeying into the woods with Bob and learned quickly how to use both a gun and a bow and arrow. Bob was impressed with her skills and didn't resist when she insisted on further training. He felt it was a means of her releasing the anger she felt deep inside in a positive manner.

Doris worried over her and often expressed her concerns to Bob at how hard she was on herself and felt she was overdoing it. Bob tempered her with the same explanation he had fed himself, so he continued to allow her to push herself to her limits physically and educationally.

They had managed to gain a fake birth certificate from the same doctor who had treated her in Clare, so they were able to ensure she received the finest education without drawing any suspicions. They made it appear she was their niece and they had adopted her after her parents died. This would prevent any further questions as to why they had a child in their home from neighbors and friends. They would be placing themselves at risk if anyone else discovered her true identity.

She recalled how she would push herself until she would either collapse from exhaustion or the blisters she received on her hands and feet would bust and bleed. She found solace in her pain and grew comfortable with it and pushed herself to obtain even greater goals by embracing it. She thirsted for knowledge and took in information like a sponge. She managed to appear happy and adjusting to her circumstances for Bob and Doris so as not to worry them since they were beginning to show signs of their age now.

She recalled how they would encourage her to make friends with other kids her age, but she shunned their diligent efforts by saying she needed to study or had already made plans. She had no desire to allow anyone else to get close enough to her, not only from fear of losing them but also she didn't wish to be influenced by them. She knew from the moment she began training what her intentions were, and she had perfected her plan over the years after much research. She had been following her soon-to-be victims through newspaper articles and records.

When she was old enough to get her driver's license, she would drive to Clare and observe them, as well as the community, without letting Bob and Doris know. She had always been careful not to be seen by anyone in the community and often disguised her appearance if she wanted to get closer. She even watched their families grow and kept close tabs on their schedules so that when she was prepared to begin enacting her revenge, she wouldn't be in for any unwanted surprises. Her intent was never to harm the innocent; rather, she wanted the guilty to personally pay for their crimes. She felt the justice system had no business in her affairs as they had not felt her pain.

The only person justified in deciding their fate was her. She felt no need to ask for their aid or their absolution. She could care less what they thought or if they believed her story. She felt they had lost nothing, so why should she allow them to financially gain from her loss? She questioned if her feelings over the judicial system would be the same had she not encountered the evil it has the potential to unleash, and she could honestly say she would still feel the same. Her thoughts on it were that they create laws they often don't live by themselves, using their positions to maneuver out of charges others might likely find themselves in prison for. She disliked how they twisted the truth to accommodate their desired outcome. She saw the system as a demonic means of controlling others for personal financial gain. Without creating victims and arresting people for doing the same things they do, their livelihood would dry up and they wouldn't be able to profit from being a natural-born liar.

She had yet to see a perfect program that truly helped people by building them up rather than enabling them and abusing them further. She was able to see what they were initially established for, but she had yet to see a perfect system even after years of their existence due to fallibility from human error or mere greed on behalf of those in a position to make effective change.

She laughed aloud as she envisioned their faces when they knew they weren't going to escape their fate and recognized the pedestals they built for themselves didn't reach high enough to make them untouchable. That was their mistake, she thought. They set themselves up for a very big fall by being overconfident and feeling too secure in their evil ways. She knew of only two absolutions—the first being we are born and the second we will all die. There was no fear of death felt by her, but she did want to finish what she came for before dying.

CHAPTER 16

D avid awoke to the sound of the alarm clock chiming and flashing at him at 5:00 a.m. He wanted to get an early start on the road so he could make it to Grand Rapids before morning traffic for his meeting with Kevin. He had explained to him the prior evening on the phone that he now had the evidence he needed to proceed with an operation to make one big swoop so that none of them had the opportunity to warn the others before they could reach them. He wanted to make certain he had them all, just as the killer had promised they would provide. It no longer mattered to him why the killer chose to help him because he wanted to take care of the much larger problem before putting his focus back on them.

After his shower and breakfast, he poured the remaining pot of coffee in his thermos and headed out for the drive. It appeared from the early morning sunrise the weather was going to be sunny and bright, making the drive enjoyable.

David thought back to the many opportunities he had turned down for promotions and transfers because he felt Gabriel needed stability and the jobs were too dangerous for him to feel he would return home and not leave his son a complete orphan. He had always felt the area was great for raising a family, with the exception of current events, which would be remedied soon with his plan. He questioned how deep this went within his own department and the community. He would soon know the extent and manpower he would need to proceed successfully, but for now, he wanted to get an idea of the direction Kevin was considering for backup. He preferred DEA, ATF, and FBI agents from western state locations, so he could be certain they wouldn't have any involvement with the other parties in the vicinity. David wasn't sure how deep this operation ran and how many law enforcement and counselors were involved. It was certainly bigger than he would have estimated within this small community. He had faith in Kevin to know who he could depend on, so he relaxed and enjoyed the sky before him through the windshield of his Jeep and turned up his stereo and enjoyed the sound of some classic rock he recalled his father listening to when he was younger. He commented out loud to himself how great the music was from the sixties and seventies. He felt the lyrics had meaning and were easily understood by the listener, and the drums and electric guitars couldn't be matched. They were masters, or so he thought. He felt he enjoyed several styles of music and was open to anything that sounded good to him.

David portrayed a lot of what some people may consider to be old-fashioned values. He felt it was important to sit down for a family meal and talk about everyone's day without the modern-day distractions of television and cellphones. He did this more often than not unless an emergency arose. He felt he needed to serve other people, but he felt quality time with his family was more valuable and important, so he left his job at the office when he returned home. He spent most of his free time with Gabriel, teaching him about life and the important qualities a man needs to possess to be considered an honorable man. He saw far too often people using televisions, gaming systems, and computers to entertain their children, and he believed they were missing opportunities to instill values in them. He felt it was utmost important to give them responsibilities and to hold them accountable for their decisions. He felt that those who have not been made to earn what they desire in life will, more often than not, never appreciate what they have been given. He felt everyone needed that opportunity to help them in building character and integrity. David tried to expose Gabriel to many different learning opportunities and experiences so that he could say he tried it, and if he liked it, David provided more opportunities for exposure and involvement.

His priority now was to get his community back in line with these values and to clean up what this group of men created. He wanted to get the problems taken care of and provide alternatives for future generations focused on character-building technics that would bring more opportunities to the community.

He had the feeling that others had seen the problem before him but feared even making a political move against this group. Things had been how they were for several decades, and the citizens became accustomed to that being their way of life. Their only other options were to leave the community and locate housing and employment elsewhere or learn to remain silent about what they knew.

David liked the size of his town and didn't want to see it change with rapid population growth but wanted to provide a steady resource of employment opportunities for those who currently resided there and had growing families. Economic growth and stability would assist in a positive outlook for the younger generations coming up. It seemed to him the people who complained the most and the loudest were the least active in assisting in affective change.

It often amazed David how those with the highest fees to their clients were the first to complain when they were asked to pay similar fees for services they received. He wondered who deluded these people into believing their services were far more valued than others, therefore are entitled to charge exorbitant fees. In regard to the legal and medical fields, he felt they were the largest legal thieves of any other service provider. He wasn't impressed when he witnessed families spending their life savings in legal fees for a loved one who had been wrongfully convicted of crimes, later to be exonerated of the crime, but not reimbursed all they had spent in legal fees. Where was the justice in that? he wondered. He felt the accusatory party should be made to pay back the wrongfully accused any expenses and lost wages incurred by the defendant, and if time were to be served, then the accuser should have to do a comparable time. That would certainly put a dent in the legal systems finances, but it would most definitely cut down on frivolous suits and accusations.

The normal law-abiding citizen is oblivious to the fact that, at any time, on any given day, they could be accused of a heinous crime and they know they are innocent, but now they're forced to prove their innocence. He often wondered who the true criminals were at times. Everything the system had been established to do had somehow been twisted and torn to the point it was almost unrecognizable. The activities of his most recent deceased victims was evidence there wasn't enough checks and balances occurring. Those in positions to do the most harm to others should be mindful of their obligations and live by the same standard they hold others to. The double standard didn't sit well with him in society or his own personal relationships. He felt it was as simple as mutual respect, which seemed to be a bygone era. His thoughts raced at the many possibilities for improving the world today, but he wasn't sure if the people would buy just how truly simple it really is.

David was nearing Grand Rapids and decided it was time to pay closer attention to his driving since he would be taking a different exit to meet with Kevin. He was amazed his phone hadn't rung yet as it usually did before he had the opportunity to make it to the office, which made him think how nice it was before the invention of cell phones. He could see where they could come in quite handy for emergency calls on the road, but they could become annoying if you allow them to control your life. He didn't like the constant access to him when he needed a day to himself or time alone with Gabriel.

"There's my exit," David spoke to himself and took the exit off to the right of the freeway. He headed toward the older part of the city into Heritage Hill Historic District. He loved the older homes and was especially impressed with the Meyer May House designed by Frank Lloyd Wright situated just up the street from his friend. The charm of a bygone era graced several street blocks with homes that had been impeccably maintained by previous and current owners. The architectural designs varied, but the craftsmanship remained top-notch. He enjoyed the walks he and Kevin had taken throughout the neighborhood, discovering the history of as many of the homes as they could each time he visited. David pulled into the driveway and pulled to the back close to the carriage house and parked. Kevin was already standing at the back door with a cup of coffee in hand for David.

"You can thank my lovely wife for this." Kevin grinned, holding the cup out as David entered the door. "She made it just how you like it. I hope you came with an appetite because she made several things for you to eat now and to take back for you and Gabriel. I tried to tell her that Mary takes great care of you."

"Yes, she does, my friend, but that lovely wife of yours has some hard-to-beat skills of her own," David complimented, taking a sip of the steaming coffee and sitting at the table where it appeared she had set a place for him. He looked down at the stack of blueberry pancakes piled on his plate with a fresh bowl of fruit on the side. He had eaten breakfast before leaving earlier, but he couldn't resist Cortney's homemade pancakes from scratch.

"Indeed she does," Kevin agreed, joining his friend for a few more pancakes of his own.

"Where is Cortney this morning?" David inquired, enjoying his first bite and looking around for any sign of Cortney or their children.

"Chase has a game tonight, so they left early to pick up the snacks for after the game," Kevin explained, delighting in his own mouthful. "She also wanted us to have an opportunity to discuss this matter privately without interruption. She's very worried about you right now. She made me promise to make sure that you were safe. I am sorry, but she forced me to tell her what was going on. You know how she can be when she notices I'm worried."

"I am not concerned about your wife revealing our plan to anyone," David confided before finishing the last bites left on his plate and cleaning up after himself. "She is no stranger to duty herself, having served this community as a prosecuting attorney."

"She is in her element no matter what she chooses," Kevin bragged on his wife. "She's a fine mother, and I am thankful she made the decision on her own to stay home with the kids. I would have supported her decision either way, but those kids certainly benefit from having her home."

"I can see that you enjoy having her home as well," David teased his friend. "We did well in our choices."

Kevin's smile seemed to wane at the mention of his friend's deceased wife, and David took note of it and explained that it did him good to remember. Kevin appeared to relax again, and they talked briefly about the things they miss the most with her being gone before getting down to the matter at hand.

David explained what he had discovered already and the approximate locations of each raid. He explained he would need several units so they could all hit their marks simultaneously. He explained to Kevin that the murderer had some link to each of the deceased, but he wasn't able to determine what it was yet but that they were providing each of the locations, and he personally confirmed they were, in fact, meth labs. He went on to explain they would likely need social services involvement if they indeed were provided the locations of several child sex slavery camps and were able to reunify children with their families. They both knew it was going to be a long road of healing for these kids from the drugs they fed them to keep them docile and the trauma of their experience. All too often they inject them with heroine to control them, which becomes addictive and prevents them from thinking clearly enough to escape. He wondered how many of them they would find still alive that had gone missing shortly after his arrival to town. He figured they would all be adults now since they were in their mid-teens when they disappeared. It will be devastating and relieving for the parents who worried night after night for a child they didn't know was alive or dead.

Neither of them could understand the darkness that had to creep into a person's heart for them to commit some of the most heinous crimes against another human, let alone children. He believed it took a very selfish person to lose compassion for your fellow man. What broke in these people that would make them believe their victims deserved their suffering was the question Kevin and David asked to each other.

Kevin had in mind several officers he intended to call on this mission. He would request a couple of renowned trauma psychologists to be available upon the discovery of any children during the investigation. He knew the numbers would grow once they made several arrests the others would leak other sources. He knew it was large, but how large, they had no idea yet.

David explained the chief had been gone for a few days, and no one had heard from him, so they would have to have an acting chief unless he appeared soon.

Kevin was aware of the size of the force in Clare as he and Cortney had visited in David's home often. They enjoyed their trips to the country where they could get away from the hustle and bustle of the busy city. He thought about how inviting it sounded at that moment.

They went over a few other plans before David was handed the bag of treats Cortney had made for him and Gabriel and made the drive back to Clare. He knew he needed to remain silent about what was about to take place since he wasn't sure who he could trust among his fellow officers. This was an insult to all the officers who took their oath to protect and serve with honor.

David hoped that Aislinn had considered his advice and thought he would give her a call to see how she was doing as he made his way into his office. The phone rang several times before going to her voice mail. He left a brief message, asking that she call him when she received his message, and went back to the data bank to see if he could come up with anything he may have potentially overlooked before going further into the file banks. He was close to having gone through the past ten years and wasn't sure if he needed to go any further.

CHAPTER 17

Aislinn had decided earlier to revisit the library and leaf through the old archives once again to see if she could find anything else that didn't seem to be quite right. She wanted mainly headlines or top stories that caught her attention. She nearly fell backward in her seat when she came across a story involving a local family who had been killed in a hail of gunfire, and it appeared the male victim had been a police officer and the others were his family. It stated that he, his wife, twelve-year-old daughter, and ten-year-old son had all been killed after the man opened fire on his fellow officers after discovering they had an open investigation with accusations of involvement in drug distribution and the manufacturing of illegal narcotics. He and his family were leaving for a family vacation, and the department feared he may have caught onto their investigation and may be fleeing, so they intercepted him on the outskirts of town where he opened fire on his fellow officers, and his family was caught in the crossfire of bullets.

Aislinn was repulsed that two innocent children died while trying to apprehend one alleged suspect. She looked further into the identities of the officers involved at the time, and a chill began at the base of her spine and ran the entirety up, causing her to shiver as though she were chilled. Two of the recent murder victims were involved in the investigation and were present during the exchange of gunfire, along with the police chief and an Officer Moran. She wondered if the recent murders could possibly be connected as a long-awaited payback. She went through other records to see if she could identify any relations to the family but was unable to identify any local relatives to either of the parents. She wanted to get as much information as possible to see if a connection could be made between the two before dismissing it as coincidence. She didn't want to bother David with any of it yet until she could dig a little deeper.

She decided to make a few stops in town to see if she could locate school photos and any other information she could gather on the children killed along with their parents. She approached several of the locals and probed into their knowledge of the town and was met with blank stares of silence when she asked about the family. It seemed they either had no knowledge or weren't willing to discuss it with her. This picked her curiosity and made her more determined to find the information she was looking for.

Aislinn could feel the hunger pains nagging at her since she had skipped breakfast and was well into the lunch hour. She decided to stop by one of the cafés and have a bite while making a couple of calls. She noticed the missed call from David when she retrieved her phone from her purse where she had placed it while visiting the library.

"Hi, David, it's me, Aislinn," she began when she heard his voice on the other end of the line. "I just got your message and wanted to check if everything is all right."

She listened to his reply and explained that she had just arrived for lunch at Mulberry Café and hadn't ordered yet. She was pleased that he had asked if he could join her since he hadn't yet eaten himself. She advised she would have a glass of water until he arrived so they could place their order together.

Aislinn caught herself daydreaming about David and allowing her thoughts to venture into areas she had never really considered before. Her thoughts strayed back to his kiss, and she could feel the warmth of his mouth pressing against hers. For the first time, she struggled fighting off the desire that burned within her to be loved by a man fully. She knew most people would never believe her if she told them she was still a virgin, but that conversation hadn't really come up before since Aislinn rarely spent time with any one person or particular group of people. She had always been too busy studying and found learning more fascinating than discussing recent fashions and the latest breakup of one of her friends. She hadn't really met anyone who she had found interesting enough to want to give up her career and freedom to spend the rest of her life with. She enjoyed her travels and carefree life too much over the years.

Until now, she hadn't given a relationship any consideration although she had been provided opportunities during her college career but chose to remain friends. She wasn't prudish or immune to intimate feelings, but she instead chose to distract herself with travels and reading. She enjoyed traveling to other countries and experiencing the culture of the people and allowing herself to connect with their daily lives to understand them more deeply. It was going to take several distant countries and other distractions to overcome the feelings she was beginning to have for David. He was everything her father would approve of and everything she could ever have imagined a man being. She told herself she was going to have to be careful with this one since it wasn't only him she would disappoint. The thought of even bringing more pain to David and Gabriel was more than she could ever fathom. They deserved more than she would be able to provide them and wanted the best for them.

"Good afternoon, Aislinn," she heard his deep voice call from behind her, nearly causing her to choke on the sip of water she had taken. "I hope I haven't made you wait too long."

"Good afternoon, David," she replied, adjusting herself in her chair to turn to see him. She nearly melted at the vision of him standing before her as the sight of him shook her to her core. He was wearing a pair of jeans that enhanced his manly physique, and she struggled to keep her eyes from straying to his manhood. It was obvious in those jeans that David was a well-endowed man, but with her lack of experience, she wondered what she knew. He wore an olive-colored pullover high-neck infantry sweater that made the green in his eyes lighter in appearance and allowed a tuft of his chest hair to show at the neckline. She hadn't noticed until now that he had a slight cleft in his chin that seemed to enhance his already-perfect jawline. She noticed the slight growth of facial hair forming into a mustache and goatee that almost made her wish she had declined lunch with him. "Has anyone told you that you are an extremely attractive man? There, I just put it out there."

"It's been quite sometime since anyone has even told me that I'm cute, but thank you," he replied, taking the seat next to her. "It's flattering to know that the most beautiful woman in the world seems to think so, and that's plenty enough for me, ma'am."

"Now that we have cleared that up," she stuttered in disbelief of her own brazenness, "how have things been going with the investigation, Detective?"

"I believe we may be getting closer to discovering our killer and their motive behind the murders, but I have some more investigating to do before I can determine the connection," he explained as he leaned in closer to her, causing prickly sensations to flow up and down her spine. "This is the beginning of something much bigger than just Clare, and I promise to give you firsthand information once I am permitted to release it."

"I appreciate that, Detective," she smiled slyly, leaning closer to his face before stopping inches from it. "I am doing a little research of my own which may be of interest to you."

"Aislinn, I thought we agreed that you were going to hold off on anything further until I know it is safe," David scolded, setting his jaw to show her his disappointment.

"I don't believe that we actually agreed," she explained, lifting her glass of water and taking a sip before continuing. "I recall you asking me not to speak with any of the families of the missing kids, but I do not recall my agreeing to halt my investigation."

"I think we should probably take a look at the menu," David stated. Reaching past Aislinn, he picked up the menu before leaning back in his chair to study it. He wasn't prepared to reply to her comment because he feared he would come off sounding like a chauvinist by making it appear she was incapable of handling her own affairs. He had no doubt she was smart and quite prepared to defend herself, but this was not your everyday investigation, and it would appear there were many more unanswered questions with any number of potential suspects. This was a long-standing and elaborate organization with many loose ends, and he needed to know she was safe.

Aislinn had intentionally baited David and was impressed with his respect of her and other women which was obvious in his need to protect, but not control. She appreciated how he made a request and not a demand regarding her career, which made him all the more attractive and appealing to her. She thought she would freely hand him over the reins to her life any day because she had no fear of him ever not having her best interests at heart.

The waitress came for their order, and it was a pleasant distraction for them both at the moment and allowed them to continue in their conversation with a change of topic. Aislinn ordered the Razzmatazz Chicken and David ordered the Pine Street Panini. The waitress returned within minutes with their drinks and salads in hand, which gave them each a few minutes to deliberate their next topic of conversation. Aislinn chose to ask about Gabriel and Mary and enjoyed the glint he got in his eyes when he talked about his son. She had no doubt that Gabriel would grow to be a fine young man, just as his father is. The time David invested in his son showed in how Gabriel carried himself. He would have no problems with the females when that time came along, she thought. She was amazed at how much he resembled David, but more so how he was like a complete replica both in physical appearance and personality.

"You seem to love children," David observed as she continued to rave over how wonderful his son is. "I am surprised you haven't decided to have your own. You'd make a great mother."

"I thought we talked about this before, but maybe I am mistaken," Aislinn began, placing her napkin on her lap after wiping the tips of her mouth. "Thank you for the compliment, but I don't feel it is appropriate for me to have a child at this time in my life since I have several years of traveling abroad and writing to do."

"Have you ever considered having a family and settling down?" David asked nonchalantly, but his insides were in knots in anticipation of her answer.

"No, to be quite honest, I haven't," she replied matter-of-factly. "I suppose I have never been asked for one, and I am never in one place long enough to establish any roots or long-term relationships. I guess you must be the only man who finds me attractive, Mr. Hough."

"That is an honest answer," he agreed before continuing, "with the exception of the last part, which I highly disagree with. I have seen men nearly fall over themselves staring at you or trying to get your attention."

"I think the detective has a flare for exaggerating the truth," Aislinn teased, taking another bite of her salad. "I am very observant and I would have noticed, but thank you for trying to build my self-esteem."

"I only state the facts, ma'am," David stated with an exaggerated voice.

"What is with the ma'am?" Aislinn asked, smiling at his reference. "I feel like an old maid when you call me that."

"I am sorry, ma'am," he replied immediately and swung his head down in an apology for slipping again. "It is a habit since childhood when speaking with a lady. I will try to be more aware because you are far from an old maid."

"I am a work in progress," Aislinn teased again, reaching her hand out to embrace his that was lying on the table. She could feel the warmth his body exuded and his smooth skin covering his hand. She wanted to leave hers there forever but pulled away after a few moments.

David stared into her eyes in hopes they would reveal something to him he longed to know but wasn't even sure what it was. Her touch had an effect on him he hadn't expected or felt in many years, so he adjusted himself in his seat to hide his discomfort. He waited a few minutes before returning his gaze back to her face and appreciating the beauty she portrayed. He seemed perplexed that someone of such beauty couldn't see it in themselves. *But maybe that is what made her even more attractive,* he mused. She was so down-to-earth and easy to talk with. He couldn't believe that any number of guys hadn't made their interest known to her. He knew how any number of men behaved in the presence of a beautiful woman and was certain she had had her share of harassment, but it didn't seem to spoil her.

"So tell me more about this investigation you are pursuing," David encouraged, trying to distract his own thoughts for the time being.

"I still have some research to complete, but it is interesting," Aislinn explained, staring back into his eyes now. "It was involving an officer and his family several years ago. The entire family died in a hail of bullets."

"Are you referring to the O'Conner family?" David asked, recalling having heard about the story from his wife and family.

"Yes, that is the name," Aislinn confirmed before asking him if he had any knowledge about them he could share with her.

"If I remember correctly, I believe he was involved in the distribution of narcotics and was a member of the Irish mafia," he explained as she waited for him to tell her something the newspaper articles hadn't already. "He had been an officer right here in Clare for, I believe, fifteen years before that day. He had married a local schoolteacher and relocated here from a small town somewhere in southern Ohio. They had a son and daughter who were with them in the car that day."

"Yes, I read that in the articles," Aislinn advised him, waiting to hear more.

"It seems that no one could believe what the paper said, and most still question how they could have been such pillars in the community and so family oriented to have had an opportunity to be living a double life," David explained, not having firsthand knowledge of the family. "I don't understand how people like that can be so willing to sacrifice the things we should hold so dearly for a few extra dollars."

"What if there is more to it and it was a cover-up?" Aislinn asked, her eyes widening to show her curiosity. "I mean, from what I read, couldn't the officers had waited to approach until he was separated from his family? It made it sound like they had this ongoing investigation and should have known if he was planning an escape."

"Would you feel better if I took a look into it after I close the books on these current affairs?" David asked, wanting to ease her look of despair and worry on her face.

"Is there a chance I might be able to take a look at the file myself?" she asked, hoping he would see it as a way of keeping her from getting too involved with his current case.

"I am not authorized to answer that, but I will check to see the classification before I can suggest other means of obtaining the information," David assured her.

"Is there someone here in town I might be able to speak with about it?" she asked, explaining she had received strange looks and silence when she asked anyone in town about it.

"That's what I was trying to explain to you earlier," David began, leaning in closer to her again. "The family was well-thought-of and loved in this town. The people are still in shock over what happened, and it probably opened some old wounds they thought they had long since forgotten."

"I sensed almost an air of shock and fear combined in each of the people I asked," she explained, just coming to that realization herself. "Why would talking about dead people bother them unless they were close to the person? Had you heard about anyone in particular they were close to, or did they have any relatives here?"

"Aislinn, I don't understand this fascination with this family when we have several murders happening right now." David looked at her quizzically and signaled her to wait on her reply as the waitress was approaching the table, and it seemed she had the bill ready. He quickly checked his watch and realized he needed to return to the office for a meeting he was scheduled to attend. "Can we possibly discuss this over dinner tonight at my place again?"

"I believe I am free for that," she replied, reaching for the bill, only to receive a disapproving look from David who had already retrieved his card and placed it in the check holder for the waitress. "Thank you again, Detective. One of these days maybe you will allow me to treat."

"Your company is payment enough." He smiled and winked. "You are a breath of fresh air in a bleak situation. Thank you for putting up with me."

"The pleasure is mine, Detective." She smiled in return and accepted the kiss he placed on her cheek before turning to leave.

"I will call you later with a time for dinner," he called behind her as he made his way from the café.

"I can't wait," she whispered low so none of the other guests would overhear.

CHAPTER 18

The stranger watched as David left the café and made his way down the quiet street to his car.

"You are a perfect creation, Detective," she said softly, slowly licking her lips as she watched him stride casually to his car, unaware of her presence. "Mmmmm, irresistibly handsome and charming. I would love to make you mine, but we can't do that, can we, Detective?"

She amused herself with his perfection until she could no longer see him before turning to find her way to the library to see if any of the papers showed a clear photo of the child victim they planted in her place since she was certainly not dead. She thought she would check to see if there were any missing girls around that time with similar features. She was going to have to get with some of her friends to see what they could find out for her.

Her first call was to one of her computer friends who knew his way inside and out of all programs and had any information at his fingertips. She shot photos of the girl to him through text and went on about seeing if she could find what Aislinn had been in search of, only she had the resources to get what she wanted, where Aislinn was held back by the very ethics she lived by. She was confined by the rules whereas the stranger felt the rules were only for those who couldn't fight their own battles. She didn't feel there was a need to ask permission for information which should be available free of charge to everyone unless someone had something to cover-up. *If it has to be hidden and forces you to lie, shouldn't you reconsider your own actions?* she thought.

She felt she was only there to remind them they are touchable and could be discovered no matter how smart or elevated in society they believed themselves to be. The regular Joe has no idea where to begin to combat these types of people, so he turns his head and pretends he doesn't see it, leading to being desensitized. For the first time, she believed she was placed on this earth to bring light to many injustices because she refused to allow them to break her all those years ago. Regardless of what others think of her means of justice, she knew she would never make it to a trial to testify if she chose that route. The road she followed led her to one-on-one confrontation where only the players involved were there to discuss the truth of the matter and to bring about true justice. She saw where turning the other cheek got her family, and she wasn't created to be that kind of believer after witnessing the devil's work firsthand.

Misery has a way of clarifying one's convictions. She didn't believe society thought things through, which, to her, was the usual norm. There will always be a few who understand the bigger picture, but for most, they allow themselves to be told what to think and how and when they should. She felt they don't take into consideration the amount of suffering an entire family is forced to endure through decisions made by others who have no clue about any of the members of that family. The system to her would always be fallible due to human error in judgment and egos. She accepted it is what it is until people stop being sheep and begin to use their own intellect. She felt others often allow their hearts to speak too quickly before allowing their brains to kick in and even once they realize they may have made an error, then their pride steps in and all chaos ensues.

She had been granted years to remember every detail of that night, without the input of others feeding her with their opinions and ideas of what had occurred as they so often do when they lead witnesses although it is illegal and unethical to do. She clearly remembered each person responsible for the crimes of rape and murder and the words they spoke. She had no one else's opinions to misconstrue the facts and details, not their facial expressions reflecting either disbelief or sympathy, and above all, she wasn't pitied, which in itself can create dysfunction in the victim's life. All those educated people who believe they have the right answers for everyone else's problems made her laugh. *That is narcissism at its best*, she thought.

"I will give you all I can, Detective," the stranger whispered, "without compromising myself. After all, I have had enough taken from me I didn't willingly give. The grief has been long and difficult, so no more for me, my dear detective. I don't expect you to understand me, and I am not asking for that. I just don't want anyone else to feel the pain, if I can prevent it for even one person."

The stranger made her way about the town, awaiting the call she had been expecting. She wanted the family of the deceased girl to know what happened to their daughter. She felt their suffering over the years with holding on to the hope their daughter would one day walk through their door. *That's the type of suffering no parent deserves ever*, she thought. As painful as discovering she would never return, at least the closure would allow them to proceed forward in their own lives. *This is where it could become tricky for me*, she thought. If she exposes the girl as not being her, will they begin a search for her again? she wondered.

"No need for that, I'm afraid." She sounded forlorn and lost momentarily. "For that little girl is also dead."

CHAPTER 19

Aislinn gathered her things after finishing her drink once David left their luncheon and made her way back to her cottage to see if one of her colleagues could help her in retrieving information about the family. She wasn't sure what it was about the case, but she had a suspicion their murder had everything to do with the recent murders. She had no idea why, but her gut told her there was a link between them, and she couldn't just ignore it despite David's warning and plea. This was her livelihood and her passion. If she allowed herself to be afraid, she could lose everything in her life she had ever hoped to gain.

Aislinn wasn't sure what the interest was in the case of the young twelve-year-old girl, but she knew she had to find the answers. She decided to distract herself by picking her clothing for the evening since she was having dinner with David. It didn't matter her mood or how her day went; she always looked forward to time spent with David and his son. They had an uncanny ability to make her smile at just the thought of them. She could feel the edges of her mouth tug upward at that very moment. She found herself surprised by her feelings for them and the connection she felt to the love they reflected for each other. It was something she craved in her own life but wasn't ready to receive. She thought for a moment and pondered if it were that she wasn't ready to receive that type of unconditional love, or did she somehow feel unworthy?

Aislinn was completely aware of the dangers in the job she did, but that didn't stop her desire to find the answers she sought. She was all about justice and truth, and she felt compelled to always seek it. She nearly laughed aloud as she thought to herself that David had a lot of nerve since his job was even more dangerous and he had a son at home. He apparently was unable to recognize his own double standard, and she would have to bring that to his attention this evening at dinner. Aislinn had no intention of being a female radical about it since that type of attack wouldn't win her support or serve to prove her point. She had no desire to be mean; she was doing it to bring awareness because she had no doubt he would completely understand what she was saying. David was not the type of man who had to show his strength by setting limits on others. She knew it was in his heart to accept other's desires in life, and he cared enough to be supportive. She had been taught that a man who was comfortable and secure in his own life could completely relate to the needs of his partner or any other woman in his life, providing the love and support she would need to pursue whatever career choice she chose. In her experiences with David, she had no doubt that he was capable of showing both strength and compassion for other people and their needs. He was a man full of confidence but never arrogant. His strength was in his character, and his character was important to him. His need to go silent over the lunch hour hadn't gone unnoticed by Aislinn, which provided her an even deeper respect for him after his superb display of self-control and desire to choose his words wisely.

"Why did you have to be so perfect?" Aislinn questioned, exasperated by her continued thoughts of him. "You make it impossible to move forward without you in my life. You are an unexpected pleasure I hadn't counted on and a distracting delight to my senses, but I have to put that aside if I even hope to successfully break this case."

Aislinn decided to go about her research for a while longer since she still had plenty of time before David would be there to pick her up. She did her best to stay focused, so when her phone rang, the sound startled her and she jumped backward in her seat before reaching for it.

She was excited when she heard her friend's voice on the other end of the phone. She had waited half the day for her friend to return the call and was happy that he had news that she had anticipated. The more her friend spoke, the more the story tied together for her. She was certain she was on the right path and was not going to be deterred or derailed by anything or anyone. She was even more determined now to go full steam ahead with her investigation to prove her hunch was more than just that.

Time had slipped by quickly between her call and her own research, and she had barely given herself enough time to get cleaned up. She made a mad dash for the shower and rinsed herself, skipping washing her hair as it took so much time to dry even with the aid of a blow-dryer.

Aislinn could feel her heart begin to palpitate and race as quickly as she did to get ready. She knew she had no intentions of sharing her newfound information with David anytime soon. She felt he had enough going on with two separate investigations, for he had not advised her that he had requested assistance from other special forces. Each was unaware of the other's knowledge, and it was her objective to keep it that way for the time being. She went back to concentrating on dressing and opted for an updo again this evening since she had no time to figure out anything else to do with her hair. She lifted it enough to allow her long, thin, elegant neck to show with her bare shoulders. She lifted the red lipstick to her mouth and dabbed at her perfect full lips. She glanced in the mirror and was surprised by her own reflection. It was rare for her to approve of her own appearance. She didn't need any critics as she was quite her own. She reached for one of her favorite perfumes and scented her wrists and neckline lightly with the soft fragrance and made her way into the living room to await his arrival.

Aislinn was able to see the front of his Jeep when he pulled up and practically ran to the door to greet him, and before he had even had an opportunity to knock, she had the door open.

"Good evening, Detective." She smiled and invited him in. "May I offer you a drink before we leave?"

"That sounds amazing right now," he agreed as he made his way through the door. "What did you have in mind?"

"I can pour you a glass of Malbec, or I can mix you a drink of your choice," she explained, awaiting his decision.

"I believe I would enjoy that Malbec, that is if you agree to have a glass also." He smiled in return.

"It seems I don't have any open, so I will give you the honor of removing the cork, if you wouldn't mind," she stated, handing him both the wine bottle and corkscrew while she retrieved two glasses for them.

She could hear the pop of the cork being removed from the bottle and turned to see him unscrewing it from the corkscrew. She held out both glasses and waited for him to pour both before handing him a glass.

Her eyes caught his, and she gazed into them a few moments before looking away and gathering her thoughts prior to speaking again.

"What has Mary decided to delight us with tonight for dinner?" she asked, trying to keep the conversation light.

"I suppose I should have asked if you enjoy Indian cuisine and allowed you to decide since some people find it spicy," David explained, hoping she would be interested in sampling it. "She's making a spicy Indian grilled chicken with basmati rice and spiced Indian cabbage."

"It all sounds wonderful," she agreed with a smile and continued. "I spent a couple of years there when I was younger. I have tried many different food from many places, but Mary seems to master each of them."

"Wow!" David exclaimed, amazed that she had spent that amount of time there. "Did your father have a career in which you traveled frequently?"

"No. I actually attended private schools in a few countries and was there alone unless they came to visit," Aislinn explained, missing the look of disbelief on David's face.

"I am at a loss for words," David began before continuing. "It must have been very difficult to send you to another country without them and the worry they must have experienced until you returned."

"It was something I chose to do myself, and they accommodated my wishes," she stated matter-of-factly. "I have always known what I wanted."

"I cannot dispute that fact at all," David agreed, smiling in agreement. "I am sure they had quite the time trying to convince you otherwise."

"Now you are catching on." She smiled slyly. "I have a way of convincing others I can handle myself."

David smiled as he recalled her quick reflexes that day by the lake. He took the seat adjacent her so that he could watch her as they talked. He had no doubt she could handle most situations, but the people involved with this case were not your average lawbreaker. These people were trained killers and had no qualms about who they were hired to kill, especially if you got in their way, and he knew that Aislinn had no problem going to extremes to prove her theory. He needed to figure out a way to keep her safe without her suspecting his interference. He seemed disappointed he was unable to find the same means he had used with others to manage his feelings for Aislinn. She had somehow managed to sneak in under his radar, and before he could react, she had made a clean getaway with his heart. Every detail about her was endearing to him—from her smile to the gleam always present in her eyes. It seemed to him that she had a world of experience but a naivete that didn't appear to go along with her experiences.

"We should probably get started toward home if you are ready," David advised as he stood to take his glass to the kitchen and placed it on the countertop.

"We wouldn't want to disappoint the chef after she has worked so hard to prepare an authentic Indian dish," Aislinn mused as she hadn't missed his reference to his home in an intimate way to her. She placed her glass next to his and followed him back to the living room where she retrieved her purse and checked to be sure her keys were inside of their usual pocket. "I believe I am ready."

David placed his hand on the small of her back as he helped her through her front door and checked to make sure the door had latched and locked behind them before taking the liberty to place it there again for the brief walk to the Jeep.

Aislinn could feel the warmth of his hand through the silk material of her dress and discovered she found herself feeling more comfortable than she had hoped to be. She slowed her gait, wanting to stroll more slowly so that she could linger in the warmth of his touch for a time. This was a new experience for her, and she wanted to bask in the pleasure he brought her because she wasn't sure if this would be the last time.

"In you go now." David smiled as he held open her door and waited for her to adjust herself in the seat before closing the door completely.

"You do realize, Detective," Aislinn began as he opened the driver's door, "I have allowed you to drive my car and you haven't once offered to provide me the opportunity to see what your Jeep can do."

He stood there for a moment before climbing the rest of the way in and responding to her complaint. The edges of his mouth drew upward into his usual half grin, and he proceeded to tease her relentlessly about how Jeeps were designed for men and that they, in no way, were meant to be driven by a female, which received him a lighthearted swat from her across his arm to which he feigned injury.

Laughter filled the vehicle as they continued their lighthearted banter the remainder of the drive.

In another life, you would have been the perfect companion for me, Detective. Just not this one, Aislinn thought as she exited the Jeep and followed him into the cabin where Mary and Gabriel awaited them.

CHAPTER 20

"Oh while I live, to be the ruler of life, not a slave, to meet life as a powerful conqueror, and nothing exterior to me will ever take command of me," the stranger quoted Walt Whitman as she paced wildly across the floor of the cabin.

She turned to look at the photo and the information her friend had sent to her in her e-mail inbox. She felt compelled to contact the family of the child they discovered had been placed in the car with her family, but she knew she could not yet or the wise detective would figure it all out before she could finish her own part.

Besides, she felt they needed to make a positive identification of the body before moving forward with that type of news to a family who had suffered many times over on numerous days. The stranger was sure that every time they heard on the news that a body of a young female had been found, they were certain it was their daughter and died another death when they discovered it was another child.

She began pacing back and forth across the floor once more; her anguish over her torn emotions made her hyper. She wanted to go after Moran, who was the last of the men present that night, but she wasn't prepared for that yet. She was livid in the beginning that her beliefs forced her to forgive what they had done to her, but she came to the knowledge that forgiveness and justice are two separate matters. The forgiveness was more so that the victim could move forward and live some quality of life and to try to lessen the pain created from the trauma.

Sometimes they can recognize what may have potentially led to the perpetrator creating the act of violence, but ultimately they made that decision and have to face the consequences of their actions. She was willing to face whatever happened even if it meant she would be executed herself for seeking her own justice rather than taking a chance on someone else to decide what their punishment should be. Those same people who would make the decision would have no concept of her suffering unless they themselves lived through similar circumstances.

She felt justified seeking her own method of justice and acting on it because she knew the price she had paid for simply being the daughter of an honorable man. It wasn't like she was murdering innocent people for the thrill of killing. In fact, she felt she was doing not only the town but also the society as a whole a justice by ridding it of the evil that preyed on them for their own financial gain. She was taught early that a man's heart will show its true origins when money is involved. They will either be controlled by their lust for it, or they will control it for the greater good of others. There was no doubt what this group of men had decided or that they destroyed countless lives. She realized some people make bad choices and realize what they had done and do their best to rectify the issue, but there are others who perpetuate and propagate to leave others with the idea these people somehow deserved what happened to them because they weren't of their class.

"You messed with the wrong one this time," she warned them under her breath. "You had all these years to prove it was a mistake, but you continued to harm others directly and indirectly with your continued crimes."

She was referring to the making and distribution of the drugs for profitable gain that stole the souls of so many users, who didn't have the strength to overcome the addiction and proceeded down a path of crime to pay for their habit. It was a vicious cycle, and the only people who generally suffer are those who are completely innocent of either crime. She noted that many people look at the addict as the problem but fail to see the creator as the main culprit, including the pharmaceutical companies and distributors of such drugs who refuse to have better research and methods of control before putting the drugs on the market. *It's an unfair advantage over those who have addictive personalities*, she thought.

Dismissing these thoughts, she decided to take a ride and to see what else she could discover for the detective. She was making preparations for a trip to Philadelphia to see what the prosecutor's brother-in-law was involved in so that she could also close down the main supplier to the area and so that they couldn't start up their business again with new people looking to make a fast buck with little to no effort on their behalf, besides taking the risk of being arrested. Hitting the manufacturers was the fastest way to slow down the distribution. No drugs, no dealers. She wasn't deluding herself into believing she was going to save the world, but she was determined to take as big of a chunk as she could out of the ones she knew of. She believed that if everyone stood in the gap and took care of the little world they lived in instead of putting their heads in the sand in hopes that someone else will take care of it, a lot more could be done to resolve the war on drugs. She was realistic in her recognition of the fact it was actually a war on greed.

She pulled across the road and watched Moran's house to see if she could see any movement from within his house. She pretended to be reading something so she wouldn't draw suspicion from any of the neighbors. She didn't plan to remain there long, but she knew that a strange car in front of your home was always a reason to have suspicion. She sat there for another thirty minutes before pulling away and driving to some of the places she knew him to frequent. She had learned that he had retired under disability from the force several years earlier when he claimed he was assaulted during an apprehension and sustained injuries, which prevented him from performing his duties as an officer. His own children were grown and no longer lived in the home, so it was him and his wife. She wondered the life that woman must lead living with such a tyrant.

Moran averaged about six feet five inches and appeared to weigh around 280 pounds from what she could estimate. He was going to be her biggest adversary from what she remembered about him. His violence knew no limits, and she wanted to have the advantage, so she took her time observing his routine. She wanted to strike when he had the least amount of favor in his advantage. Even a bullet, unless directed in two primary locations, wouldn't stop him from overtaking her if she weren't careful.

She drove to Mount Pleasant just south of Clare and pulled into the parking lot where she saw his truck sitting across the street from the Bird Bar and Grill. She had followed him here on several occasions prior to this day, so she had a pretty good guess that is where she would find him. She waited for a few minutes before deciding to step inside and look around. She caught a glimpse of him sitting at the bar and decided to take a table at the opposite end where she hoped the dim lighting would prevent him from getting a good look at her. She hadn't had her dinner, so she ordered something light from the menu and a beer when the waitress approached her. Without the menu to cover her, she took out her phone and brought it up to her face to block his ability to see her fully.

Moran was laughing heartily with a couple of guys who looked like regulars. She didn't feel he would be departing soon since he had just ordered another beer, so she slid into the restroom and placed a call before returning to her table. She slid back into the seat and would glance up on occasion to see if anyone else had joined them. She shot a few photos of the other men so she could check to see if they could be identified or possibly affiliated with Moran. The quality was poor due to distance and lighting, but her friend was very good at bringing in the details. She pressed the Send button as the waitress approached the table with her dinner and placed her phone back into her purse.

She ate slowly and enjoyed her meal, only glancing up when someone came in or left the bar. She could hear Moran telling the other guys he needed to head up the road, so she motioned for the waitress to bring her tab, and after paying, she went back to her car and waited for him to leave. She watched as he exited the door and walked across the street to his truck. He didn't start the engine immediately. He appeared to be dialing a number on his phone as he sat there behind the wheel. Several minutes later, she could hear the rumble of the dual exhaust system as he started the truck and pulled from the curb. She pulled her car to the edge of the parking lot and allowed another car to proceed before turning in the same direction.

She was able to see his truck ahead of the SUV as Moran steered over the center line a few times before pulling it back into his lane.

The SUV remained between them for the next seven miles before turning onto a side road, leaving only road between her and Moran now. She let off the pedal to leave an even bigger gap between them, hoping another car would pass her, but Moran turned his signal on and made a left-hand turn onto a narrow dirt road that didn't appear to have much traffic. She passed it and slowed down, hoping to see a place she could pull off or another road she could possibly turn down so that she could hike back to see what he was up to. Unable to find anything close, she turned the car around and drove back toward the road she had seen him turn on. No cars were coming in either direction, so she pulled to the side of the road near the entrance and looked down the road to see if she could still see his truck. The road seemed to veer to the right about a hundred yards in, and with the foliage, she was unable to see where it went from there. Wanting a closer look, she stepped from her vehicle and started to walk down the edge of the drive, believing she would hear the truck if he were to head back toward the road. She wasn't sure how far back in he had driven, but she would go as far as she needed to in order to get a good view. She hadn't made it to the tree line when a vehicle pulled behind her and a couple of shady men stepped out of their car and asked what she was doing.

The stranger turned in their direction and walked toward them as she concocted a story she thought they would buy.

"I lost an important document out my car window, and I am trying to locate it," she explained, keeping herself calm. "I rolled it down without thinking to get some fresh air and the wind caught it. I really need to find it."

"Important, huh?" one of the guys asked.

"It's very important," she replied, pretending to still search.

"What are you, an attorney or something?" the other asked.

"You figured me out." She smiled and continued to walk toward her car.

"You're too pretty to be an attorney," the first guy spoke again.

"I wasn't aware there were stipulations on looks pertaining to the field," she replied, getting closer to her car. "It must have blown farther up the road."

"We could help you look, but it will cost you," the other guy stated with an evil smile on his face as he made his way in her direction.

"I don't want to take any of your time. I am sure I can have it resent," she declined, walking faster now.

He stepped up his pace, and she found that he had caught up with her before she could open her car door.

"We have all of the time in the world, especially for someone as pretty as you," he replied, reaching his hand up to touch a lock of her hair.

"Thanks, but I am out of time and will have it resent. I appreciate your offer," she replied, trying to remain calm as she pulled at the door handle. She started to open the door, and he pushed it closed before she could step into her car.

"When a man offers to help, you should accept his offer," he snarled as his voice changed tones, and he closed the gap between them and pressed himself against her, forcing her back against the car.

"As I explained, I am really in a hurry," she stated, showing no fear of his aggressive behavior. "Thanks, but no thanks."

"Did you hear this sassy little thing?" he asked his friend in a mocking gesture to her. "She don't like us, Gerald. I think she thinks she's too good for us."

"Listen, I don't want any trouble," she started, trying once again to open the door, but he held it tight.

"We don't plan to give you any trouble, little miss. We aim to please," he taunted, pressing his body firmly against hers. "Ain't that right, Gerald?"

"You better leave the lady alone, Mark. She don't want no trouble," his friend called to him. "Besides, the boss is waiting for us. We need to get going."

"Well, maybe she would like to join us for a little fun. I am sure he would appreciate her company," he responded, still pressing against her. "Come on, I think you would enjoy it."

"Please, I asked you nicely," she replied softly, adjusting her body so that she could get a firm stance.

"And I asked you nicely. Now I'm telling you," he growled as he grabbed her arm and tried to pull her toward their vehicle.

The stranger brought her knee back and met his groin area with a sharp upward motion that caused him to bend over and scream in agony, and as he went forward, she brought her foot up to meet his face with a force so intense she could hear the bones crunch before the blood crept from his nose and mouth. She could see his friend moving swiftly toward them and decided she had enough time to get in her car before he reached them. The injuries didn't prevent him from reaching out and grabbing her leg, causing her to kick him again until he released her. His friend was gaining on her quickly, but she was able to slide into the driver's seat and hit the Start button as she pressed on the brake, and within a couple of seconds, she slammed the gear shift into Drive and hammered the gas pedal to the floor, causing the car to slide back and forth in the gravel. She felt a bump and heard the scream from the one still lying on the ground as it appeared she had run over one of his legs.

The two front tires grabbed at the pavement, and she spun the wheel in the direction of Clare and accelerated to put as much distance between her and them. She could see in her rearview mirror the other man grabbing his friend and lifting him from the ground. She didn't let off the gas until she was sure there was no way they would catch up to her before she made it to her turn off.

She muttered under her breath at her frustration in herself for not having been more cautious and not thinking ahead that someone else could be meeting him there. She had a lucky break that they weren't armed with anything but ignorance; otherwise, the outcome could have been entirely different than it had been. She was so close to achieving what she had come for and couldn't afford to make a mistake that would prevent her completing it. She headed back in the direction of her father's cabin with the intention of taking the dirt bike out, instead of her car, so she could return without them seeing her. She decided she would cut through the woods close to the area and hike the rest of the way until she found what she was looking for. She had no doubt this was another meth lab since the other guys were there to meet with Moran.

The stranger went inside once she arrived and quickly changed her clothes into something more suited for the woods and pulled her hair into a ponytail. She gathered together her supplies, which included a gun with a full clip, binoculars, and her camera. It would have been easy for her to recognize the men who tried to accost her, but that meant she would have to pick them out of a lineup, and she knew that wouldn't happen without revealing her identity. Photos would serve the same purpose, especially ones that revealed what they were doing. She placed the items in a backpack and headed to the shed to get the dirt bike. She filled the fuel tank with the remaining gas from the gas can nearby to be certain she would not run out and secured her pack on the back of the bike before starting it. She kicked the bike in gear and made her way back to the location of the road, hoping they had not already left the site. She passed by the drive and could notably see her tracks from earlier where she spun out. She decided to come in from the other direction this time and cut into the woods several yards from the drive.

Halfway in, she retrieved her binoculars and looked to see if she could see any signs of them or a building. She caught a glimpse of what appeared to be a structure, so she killed the motor and grabbed her pack from the back before heading in the direction she thought she saw the building in. She made her way quietly through the woods, checking her surroundings in case they had people scouting the area. She climbed a small hill, and when she reached the top, she pulled out the binoculars and scanned the area.

"Well, now what have we here?" she mused once she caught sight of what appeared to be a block building covered in camouflage netting to conceal it from helicopters or planes flying overhead approximately fifty yards ahead of her. She would have likely missed it had she not heard Moran's voice booming out orders to the two men she had encountered earlier on the road. She laughed inside as she zoomed in on the guy's face and could see the swelling and traces of blood where she had clearly broken his nose. She took the camera from the backpack and placed her largest lens on so she could zoom it in directly on them since she was unable to get closer without being detected and snapped several shots.

"Wait a minute. What is this?"

She sat up and adjusted her eyes to make sure she was seeing what she thought she saw. Sure enough, they had two females who appeared to be in their late teens bound and gagged and were placing them in the back of a cargo van. She quickly snapped off as many shots as she could in hopes of getting a clear enough photo for the girls to be identified. She zoomed in on the license plate of the van and took several more.

"So this is where you hide them before taking them elsewhere," she whispered, wondering how many more were inside. There was no way she could intervene and help the girls at this time. She thought about calling it in but wasn't sure it would do any good since she had no idea who she could trust from the department. It could create more problems for the girls if she didn't follow them instead and wait until they reached another location.

"Don't fuck this up, Mark, with your stupidity, or I am likely to end your miserable life myself," Moran warned, shoving him in the direction of the van. "I expect you to keep that idiot in line, Gerald, or it's your ass. Just get them there and then get your asses back here immediately. We have a lot to take care of."

"I got this, boss," Gerald replied as he climbed into the driver's seat of the van and awaited his friend who was limping still from his previous encounter.

She placed everything back into the pack and hurried back to her bike. She jumped on and headed back in the direction of the road where she stayed deep enough in the woods not to be seen. She watched as they turned left onto the main road and passed her before she cut out and onto the road behind them and maintained a safe distance as she tried to figure out what she needed to do to help the two girls. She followed them through a couple of smaller communities until they came to Pine Haven Recreational Area where they pulled off. She presumed this was where they planned to meet whoever they intended to hand the two girls over. She knew she would be unable to follow the remainder of the drive since she hadn't been able to stop to refuel, so she pulled to the end of the parking lot and decided now was the time to intercede if she expected to be of any help to the girls. She pulled the gun from her pack and cocked it to load a bullet into the chamber and placed it beneath her sweatshirt and proceeded in their direction. She pulled her hood up on her sweatshirt to conceal her face from them as she got closer. She crouched behind the van and reached up to try the door at the rear of the van, hoping they hadn't locked it from the inside. The handle slid down, and she could feel the door release but waited to pull it open until she was able to pull the gun from the waist of her pants. She took in a deep breath, and in one swift motion, she jerked open the door and jumped into the back of the van.

"What the—" was all Gerald got out before she had the gun to the side of his head.

"Do not move or even breath," she warned, forcing the gun deeper into the side of his head. "Tell your friend there to remain calm, or I will be forced to splatter your pea brain all over this windshield before turning it on him."

"You're that bitch from earlier today," his partner muttered through his busted mouth as he attempted to turn in his seat and move in her direction. "You must have a death wish, you little cunt."

"Apparently your friend doesn't care whether you live or die," she warned, pressing her finger against the trigger halfway. "You have two seconds to comply."

"Do what she says," Gerald warned his friend in a panicked voice. "What do you want?"

"That's much better," she coached, turning to his friend. "I want you to first take these cuffs I am going to hand you and place them on your friend over there with his arms behind his back and then you are going to untie these girls and do exactly as I tell you to."

She handed him the set of handcuffs and watched as he put them over each wrist. She leaned in to secure them as tight as they would go until he whined about them cutting into his flesh. She told him to climb through the middle of the van and watched as he undid the gags from the girls' mouths and released the duct tape they used to bind their wrists together. Both girls whimpered and cowered away, clearly traumatized by their current situation.

"Girls, I am going to need for you to calm down and give me a hand here," she spoke softly, handing one of them another set of cuffs. The girl shrank away from her and held tight to the other. "Come on, sweetie, I really need you to do this. I am not going to hurt you."

The girl reached for the cuffs and did what she was directed to do by cuffing his hands behind his back like his partner.

"Now I am going to need you to help me get them out of the van and over to that tree right there," the stranger explained as she pulled the van closer to her motorcycle and pointed in the direction where she wanted them. Both girls complied and pulled at the two men to remove them without drawing too much attention from anyone else in the area.

The idiot who had tried to take liberties with her earlier started to get loud, so she took the tape and covered his mouth after smashing the butt of her pistol against his already-fractured nose. She could hear the muffled groans through the tape.

She had the girls secure their hands with their backs against the tree so they wouldn't be able to free themselves without help and then asked them to help her load the bike into the back of the van.

She walked back to the two men and explained that she really wanted to rid the earth of their existence, but she felt they would have a much more difficult time adjusting to prison life once they were convicted of the abduction and aiding in sex slave trade of minor children.

"Let's go, girls," she ordered, explaining they needed to get out before the others who they were meeting showed up. She drove the girls to the nearest gas station so that she could refuel her bike for the drive back and made a call to the local authorities and so that the girls could be picked up safely and returned to their families. She bought them food from inside the market and told them to remain there until the authorities came, assuring them they would be safe. She asked if there were others in the building they were held in, and they told her there were at least five other girls and a couple of younger boys still there. She planned to keep a close eye on the place to make sure they didn't try to relocate them after today's incident.

The two girls were not from the area and had been brought here from other states. One had been missing for a couple of months from Ohio and the other young lady was from Illinois. She told them not to mention her but to take credit in overcoming the two men themselves and escaping by taking their vehicle.

The stranger waited nearby and watched as the police pulled in with sirens blaring before proceeding back to the cabin where she could finish putting together her final plan for Moran. She would add the location of the building she had located and pray the detective moved quickly before Moran had an opportunity to relocate the others.

She had hoped for more time but realized her time had drawn nigh. She would have to work double time if her plan was to be successful. She mapped the latest find on the outline she intended to send to the detective and placed it in the envelope for delivery and drove to the post office in Mt. Pleasant where she dropped it in the mailbox outside of the post office.

"It's all up to you now, Detective," she spoke out loud to herself as she made the drive back to the cabin so she could rest for a spell before the big finale.

CHAPTER 21

David stopped by the doughnut shop and grabbed a cup of coffee on his way to the office. He spoke briefly with some of the locals before heading in the direction of the office. He no sooner sat down at his desk than one of his fellow officers knocked on his door and asked if he had a minute to discuss the disappearance of the chief.

David had nearly forgotten the chief hadn't returned with everything else going on and was advised by the officer that they had contacted his family and close friends, and none of them had seen or heard from the chief. He asked the officer if anyone had taken the liberty of driving to the chief's cabin to see if he was possibly there since they had apparently exhausted all other possibilities.

"I guess we hadn't thought about that, sir," the officer replied, looking sheepish that they hadn't considered that a possibility.

"Send an officer to check it out," David ordered, going back to the file he had been reviewing. "Let me know if anything turns up."

"I will drive out with Cutright and see if he is there," the officer informed him on his way out the door, closing it behind him.

David went back to the file when another knock interrupted him again.

"Come in," David ordered, sounding testier than he had intended.

"Another package came for you, and I wanted to make sure you received it," Pam advised, handing the package to him. "It says it's important on the front of the envelope, so I thought I would bring it to you personally."

"Thanks, Pam. I appreciate that," David praised, taking the package from her and tearing the seal open. He removed the contents, and before opening it further, he recognized it as the information from the killer he had been promised. He leafed through the written letter before reviewing the map in detail. He immediately dialed Kevin and asked if they could meet somewhere close so that he could provide him the details of what had been given to him. He stressed the importance of moving quickly since the location of the kids had been provided.

"Did you hear about the two girls who escaped from their abductors and were picked up near Midland?" Kevin asked. "It appears it may be a direct link to our investigation."

"No, I hadn't heard," David replied, wanting to hear more.

"They are being held there for their protection until they can get the full story and contact the families. It isn't far from where they located two of the men responsible who had been bound to a tree in a park area not far from Midland. They are insisting there was a third female involved, but the girls are denying the men's stories," Kevin continued, explaining that he felt David needed to strike while the iron was still hot.

"I am leaving now, so please let them know I am on my way and I will need full cooperation from their staff," David requested, grabbing the envelope from his desk to provide to Kevin when he arrived. "This could be the break we needed, Kevin."

He placed the phone back in its cradle and headed out the door to make the drive to Midland. His excitement that they may have finally received the break they needed to not only rid the town of the lowlifes who preyed on the weaker, but he also could have a possible identity of the killer if what the two men claim is true. What purpose would they have to claim there was a third person, and what could be gained by the two female victims who escaped to lie about what had actually transpired? He wondered. He had every intention of uncovering the truth once he was able to speak with all parties.

David was anxious to get there as quickly as possible, so he turned on his lights and siren and drove at a high rate of speed, cutting the time of the drive. He pulled into the lot of the police department and practically ran to the entrance door of the station. Inside, he explained to the desk clerk his business there and was asked to take a seat while they contacted their chief.

"Good morning, Detective," the chief greeted as he approached David. "I got a call informing me that you would be arriving today."

"Thank you for meeting with me," David replied, standing to shake the chief's hand. "I understand you have the two females in custody still."

"Yes, but we placed them in a safe house until we can figure out what is going on," he informed David. "The two perps are here, if you would like to start with them."

"I see no reason why I can't start there since they are available now," David agreed and followed the chief to his office.

Inside the chief's office, he turned to David and asked him to have a seat and offered him a cup of coffee, which David gladly accepted.

"What the hell are we dealing with here, Detective?" the chief asked.

"This situation is much bigger than I had originally suspected, sir, and I am not sure how many people are involved as of yet, but I can tell you I am in a predicament of not knowing who I can trust since some of the people involved are officers and court officials," David advised, taking a sip of his coffee before continuing. "I have a couple of dead cops and prosecutor, and it appears they are involved in much more than just trafficking drugs as you are aware of with these to young ladies in your care."

"Are you referring to sex trafficking of children?" the chief inquired.

"I do believe that might be the case," David suggested. "I think we will know more once we've had the opportunity to talk with the alleged perpetrators and the two girls."

"I don't know how these girls managed it, but they did a number on one of them." The chief snickered. "We had to take him for medical treatment before booking him in."

"That does seem a little odd," David agreed.

"Let me get them transferred to the interrogation room, and we can get started if you're ready," the chief advised.

"I am ready when you are, Chief," David replied, standing to follow the chief through several corridors to the designated room.

They stood on the other side of the one-way glass and watched as they brought in the first guy. The chief explained they would start with him before bringing in his partner. He provided David with as much background information they could find on the guy before entering the room together.

"Mr. Williams, this is Detective Hough from the Clare Police Department. He has a few questions he would like to ask," the chief informed Gerald. "Do you have any reservations about talking with him?"

"No, I will see what he has to say," Gerald replied, sitting back in the chair and placing his hands on top of the table.

"Thank you for allowing me the opportunity to hear your side of the story," David said before sitting down across the table from him. "If you don't mind, I would like to hear your side of what happened before I ask any questions."

"Whatever floats your boat, Detective," Gerald replied sarcastically. "Not that it makes much difference."

David asked Gerald if he would like some coffee or water before he proceeded with his story.

"I'll take a coffee. Black," Gerald insisted before continuing his version of what happened and how the girls came to be in his cargo van. He figured there was no point in lying now since the two girls would be considered strong and credible witnesses. When he concluded his story, he leaned back in the chair and told the detective to fire away with his questions.

David paused for several minutes, digesting everything he had heard before proceeding with his first question.

"Did I understand you correctly when you said there was a third party, a female, who you had an earlier encounter with who followed you to the park and overtook you and Mr. Snyder while you were waiting for the people you were sent to meet?" David inquired.

"You heard me right," Gerald insisted.

"Can you give a description of what she looked like?" David asked, hoping he could get a visual idea of what she looked like.

"Her looks were definitely not what you see from the average female," Gerald informed him. "She's a looker and easy on the eyes, but she is one badass bitch."

"Can you give me a description of her physical appearance?" David asked, seeming a little agitated over his attitude of women.

"Yeah, she looked to be the professional type, not your average female. Like I said, she's a real looker," he repeated. "She has long dark hair and is tall and thin, but she has a real nice body, if you know what I mean."

"Is there anything else about her you can recall?" David urged, hoping to get some more identification. "Could you see the color of her eyes? Was she Caucasian? Or are there any other identifying characteristics that could help identify her?"

"She was a white girl, but I couldn't see her eyes because she kept her hood pulled over her head, so I wasn't able to get a good look," he replied, acting like he was tired of the questions.

"Thank you for your help, Mr. Williams," David added with an air of dismissal. "I may have further questions later for you."

"Yeah, yeah, whatever you say," Gerald smarted off before standing to be led back to his cell by the officer standing by the door. "You had better find that little bitch before my boss does, or you won't have to worry about her anymore."

David ignored the threat and watched as they led him from the room. He and the chief chatted briefly before they brought in Mr. Snyder. David looked at the chief after seeing the obvious injuries on his face.

The chief went through the same introductions he had with Mr. Williams, who was also willing to share what he knew about the days' events.

"That looks painful," David started out, getting a closer look at the damages to his face inflicted by the female Gerald described.

"It's nothing compared to what I am going to do to that little cunt when I find her," Mark warned with a look of determination on his battered face.

"Who are you referring to?" David asked, knowing what the answer was he would provide.

"That bitch who interfered in our business," he continued. "She has no idea what is about to take place when they find her."

"When who finds her?" the chief interjected.

"Never mind that pig," he snarled with a look of hatred in his eyes that now had dark rings formed around each eye.

"Had you ever seen this woman before today?" David asked, hoping he could make a connection to an area.

"I ain't never seen her before, but she will be sorry when I run into her again," he confided. "She is easily identifiable. Not many bitches have her looks."

"You seem to have a deep-seated dislike for females, Mr. Snyder. Is there a reason for that?" David asked, looking him in the eyes.

"They are only good for two things—fucking and taking care of my needs," Snyder replied with a disgusted look on his face.

"That's a pretty distorted view of women you have," David interjected. "Does it relate back to your own mother?"

"That whore died from being unable to control her heroin use. Serves the bitch right. She was never a mother," Snyder spewed, but David could see the anguish in his eyes from a lost childhood. This didn't excuse the cruelty he inflicted on other innocent people by his miscued beliefs about all women.

"Can you give me a description of the woman who assaulted you?" David asked, hoping he could offer a more detailed picture of what she looked like.

"Yeah, she had long dark hair and a face and body for fucking. She had those perfect lips good for satisfying a man's needs. You know, the full lips. Her nose was little and upturned a bit, and her eyes were a color I hadn't seen before," he continued his description. "She's about to lose all that when they slice and dice that pretty little face."

"You do realize that you are making threats to do bodily harm to another person and could incur further charges, don't you?" David warned as he became more disgusted with this piece of shit.

"Do I look like I give a good fuck, you dick?" Snyder argued. "Don't pretend you are above the same feelings. I know all men want only one thing from these bitches."

"Get this moron out of my sight," David insisted as he stood to leave the room. "You're a pathetic excuse for a human being, Snyder, and a very sick man."

"Fuck you, pig. You'll die along with her when it is all said and done!" Snyder screamed as he resisted the officer who was there to return him to his cell. "I might even personally give it to you up that tight ass of yours."

David turned back toward him and told him he couldn't wait for the day for him to try before exiting the room with the chief.

"Those two are something else," David told the chief, but in the recesses of his mind, he could only think of one person that fit their description, but there was no way it could be her. He couldn't see Aislinn having the ability to do what was done. She was a gentle soul whom he felt could never think to hurt another person as far as he could see, but her physical beauty did by far exceed most other females.

"They are those whom I feel have no hope of being rehabilitated, yet we are forced to take care of their needs while they are here," the chief complained. "They are too far gone to ever have a change in their hearts that could ever be beneficial to society. They prey on the weakest and have no remorse for their actions."

"Can we speak to the young ladies now?" David asked, anxious to hear what their version was. "Those men made her appear to be some kind of superhero with special powers, which we all know are made-up stories. I think they don't want to admit they were outdone by two kids."

"I can give you a ride over to where we have them," the chief explained. "We would like to get them back to their families soon, and we are working to be absolutely sure they are who they say they are before contacting who they claim to be their parents. We have done some checking into their stories, and so far everything seems to be on the up and up. We hope to contact the parents today and see if they can make the trip up to provide a positive ID before releasing the girls."

David entered the safe house with the chief and noticed the two girls seemed to huddle beside each other even though they were removed from the nightmare in which they had been living for the past several months. He could only imagine the hell they had been living with these animals disguised as humans and found solace in the company of the other who had lived their fate. He approached them and asked if they would be willing to talk with him. Both girls nodded their heads but remained silent until he began his questioning.

"I understand you ladies have been through a lot recently, but anything you can tell me may also help any others who are still in the situation you ladies found yourselves to be." David spoke softly with understanding. "We would like to get you back with your families as soon as possible, but we really need your help right now to help the others. Are you willing to share everything you know, or are you comfortable with that?"

One of the girls spoke up and said they wanted to do everything they could to help the others who were still at the location they were being moved from. They told David there were others who had been taken before they came for them, and they didn't know where they had moved them or if they were even still alive. They told of the horrors they had lived and witnessed where others had been tortured and killed in front of them, and they supposed it was to keep them compliant with their demands.

David's heart cried out for the girls, but he maintained his composure as he listened to everything they told him. He waited until they felt they had shared everything they could remember before asking questions about how they had managed to escape the two men. He took note of the silence from each of them regarding their escape.

"Ladies, the only way we can guarantee your safety and resolve this matter is if you are completely honest about what happened," David explained. "I am baffled as to how either of you could have removed your own restraints and overtaken both men without any type of weapon. Can you tell me which of you did that?"

Both girls looked at each other with confused expressions and weren't sure what to say, so they both remained quiet.

"There was someone else there, wasn't there?" David insisted, looking at each of them. "It's all right to tell me because neither one of you did anything wrong, and if it weren't for this person, you may not be here to tell us what happened. We aren't upset about what she did. In fact, we would like to personally thank her for her bravery. It isn't every day that people go out of their way to place themselves in a dangerous situation to help a total stranger."

One of the girls finally spoke up after several minutes of silence. Her description was similar to how both men described her, but they added they believed she was an angel sent to answer their prayers. Their description of her not only described her physical beauty, but they truly felt she also had superhuman powers in order to overtake both men as she had.

"She asked us not to tell anyone else about what she did and that we should say that we had a lucky break and were able to get away when they weren't watching."

"That would leave out the part where they were bound to a tree, if you had merely escaped, wouldn't it?" David explained, trying not to sound condescending to the girls. "The story didn't add up, and that's why it is important that you give us any details you can remember about what happened."

The girls concluded their story with the actual facts of what had occurred and explained they helped her tie the men to the tree before loading her motorcycle into the van where she drove off after leaving them at the gas station where they were picked up by an officer and brought here.

David thanked both of the girls and asked the chief if he would let him know when they had been returned to their families safely. The chief assured him he would do that and would also make sure they received the proper services to help them overcome their traumatic experience in hopes they could live a normal life.

David knew that a trial would be just as traumatic, and he prayed the courts would be sympathetic to their needs and not allow further exploitation of them. He also advised they be provided protection until after the trial concluded. He wanted to tell them that everything would be all right, but he knew it was going to be a long road for both of them to reach a point of healing.

He followed the chief back to his office while they awaited Kevin's arrival so they could discuss a plan to retract the other children without tipping off the others before they were prepared to make their countywide sweep. They felt this could be handled by local authorities to prevent the others from becoming suspicious. They would play it up as though the girls had an opportunity to escape and took it.

Kevin and David kept the other matters under their hats while in the presence of the chief since it had nothing to do with the current situation as far as the chief was concerned. They asked that he keep a closer watch on the park area since this appeared to be a transfer area, which he readily agreed he would do. They thanked him before departing to find a place they could discuss the details of their plan in private. David gave Kevin a copy of everything that had been given him by the killer. Kevin felt they had enough to begin aligning the date they would initiate the raid. They would have several teams to cover each of the locations they had discovered. Satisfied they had everything they needed, they parted ways, and David made the drive back to Clare.

David thought about the description both victims gave of the woman who rescued them, and he couldn't help but to visualize Aislinn since their description reminded him of her. He himself thought of her as one of the most beautiful women he had seen, and he couldn't deny that she reminded him also of an angel, but for different reasons than they described. He questioned why she was always on his mind since the first day he met her in the coffee shop. He found her to be one of the most interesting and intriguing people he had encountered and wanted to know everything there was to know about her, but the more he learned about her, it seemed the less he knew. She was an enigma he was compelled to learn more about as soon as he was able to close the case he was working on he would give her more attention.

CHAPTER 22

Aislinn had spent the morning checking flight prices to Philadelphia since the drive would take too long from her current location. She would book the flight out of Grand Rapids rather than Detroit since she liked the area better. She thought she would spend a couple of days catching some of the art which was so prevalent to the area before flying out.

She felt she needed to put some distance between her and David so that she could get better control over her feelings for him, which seemed to be clouding her ability to focus on her job. He had somehow managed to change some of her views on her own goals and life ambitions. She had not anticipated this and definitely hadn't invited it; after all, she had her career she had worked diligently to build, and Clare wasn't exactly her ideal place to live since she preferred larger cities. She wasn't even sure if she would remain in the states although she would retain her citizenship. There were yet places to be seen that she had not visited, and she didn't need the guilt that would accompany a relationship if she chose to venture off for months at a time in another country. She would have to decline any invites David offered or she would never be able to leave when it was time. Her feelings for him were more than she wanted to let go as it was, and she did not want to hurt him any more than he had already been. He was too good for that and deserved much more than she could possibly provide for him and Gabriel.

Aislinn wanted to get an interview with retired officer Moran before she made the flight regarding the occurrence with the dead officer and his family since he was the only person left who might provide her insight into what happened that day. She knew David would be livid, but this was her life and career, and he would simply have to understand that is how investigative journalism works. Every career has its good and bad, and maybe hers carried a few more risks when the job is done correctly, but nonetheless it was her livelihood and passion.

She was going to follow her gut on this, and in her heart she knew the recent murders were somehow connected to the death of the family she had uncovered. There was something not right with how they died, and she wanted to find out exactly what happened that day since all the records her friend was able to hack didn't add up to the description each of the officers testified and witnessed to. She wondered if Moran was worried since everyone else there that day had already died, at least she knew that if it were her, she would be.

Aislinn decided to take a drive to the address listed for him to see if he would be willing to sit and have a conversation. She pulled in front of the house on the street curb and made her way up the walk to the front door of the house. She pressed the doorbell and waited to see if she could hear any noise from inside the house. Within a few moments, she could hear footsteps coming in the direction of the door from inside and could tell she was being observed from the peephole through the door. Within a few seconds, she heard the door seal break as a woman appeared through the open door.

"Can I help you with something?" Mrs. Moran asked as she looked at Aislinn, who stood on the porch.

"Hi, ma'am," Aislinn began before continuing. "I was wondering if this is the home of Mr. Robert Moran, and if it is, would he have a few minutes to speak with me?"

"What's this regarding?" she asked, still not saying if he was there.

"Well, ma'am, I am a reporter, and I was hoping to have the opportunity to speak with him pertaining to a matter that took place several years ago with one of his fellow officers," Aislinn explained, hoping she would allow her inside, but the look on the woman's face told her that wasn't likely to happen. In fact, the look turned to one Aislinn would have regarded as shock and fear just before she hurried back inside and slammed the door in Aislinn's face.

Aislinn stood there for a few moments trying to understand what had just taken place before turning to go back to her car, and as she was about to climb inside, she heard the voice of the woman call a warning to her that she just needed to go on and not bring up such things. She told her to leave before something bad happened and closed the door once more. Unable to respond or speak to the woman again, Aislinn climbed inside her car, and on the drive back to the cottage, she asked herself what this woman knew that would frighten her and cause her to think something would happen to her. Did she know the truth of what happened to that family? Had he confided in his wife the story of what took place during the massacre? Aislinn had to find him so that she could see if he would be willing to tell what he actually knew.

She decided she would have to watch his activities and see if she could find an opportunity to speak with him with no one else around. She paced the floor anxiously, trying to figure out what she needed to do next and if she had somehow placed herself in a bad situation, from the reaction of what she presumed to be Robert Moran's wife whom she spoke with. From the look in the woman's eyes, Aislinn thought she looked as if she had seen a ghost or something unnatural.

"That's all right. He has to come home sometime," Aislinn groaned, not having obtained the information she had hoped to this visit, but she was sure she would be coming back soon. She knew she would have to park somewhere else and walk around when she returned since his wife now knew her car. She decided to hang around town for a while in hopes of running into Mr. Moran by chance and made a couple of passes by the house before returning to her cottage later empty-handed.

CHAPTER 23

David and Kevin recapped their plan with the other men they would be working with during the operation. They had to move things up with the recent event that occurred in case it caused a chain of events of others running into hiding out of fear that Gerald and Mark had decided to take a plea and turn state's evidence against them. They had hoped to have more time to execute their plan to see if they could identify the other location where they were keeping any of the other kids they had taken. They wanted to make sure they didn't place them in any higher danger than they currently were or risk them being moved before they could retrieve them.

They set up their observation of each location to see if they would try to move their equipment or the kids and destroy any of the evidence they could gather on them. This meant they would have to camp near each of the sites and keep watch for twenty-four hours and move if they had to. They took note of all the vehicles coming and going from each of the locations as another means of identifying anyone potentially connected to the illegal operation.

David was almost certain it would also provide him an opportunity to discover the killer's identity. He had a feeling they wouldn't be able to sit idly by and allow the police to do their job. They had too much at stake to permit any mistakes to be made on the department's behalf. He felt that the killer had taken years to plan their killing spree. They had to have had patience and the desire to make sure they had enough time to execute it to their perfection. He mused at the thought that the killer's tenacity was to be admired, and he believed they weren't of average intellect. They had managed to go undetected by any of the locals or those involved in any of the illicit activities, which led him to think maybe they were within close proximity, but not residing in Clare. It still picked at his curiosity why they would take so many years to execute their plan but then risk everything to help complete strangers. That was the part which he struggled to understand. He had a feeling that would be the part that would get them caught, and he hoped to be there to find out why they did what they did so that he could possibly have a better understanding how people can be led to commit the crimes they do.

David knew the usual motives were power and greed, and those things could drive a man to lose his mind if not kept in balance, but these murders weren't for personal gain, rather an act of vengeance. This person would not be content with the mere arrest of those dead, and that message was made very clear. They had taken something very valuable away from this person, and David could only think of one thing he would kill for and that was his son and his deceased wife, along with his parents and people he loved. He would not hesitate if someone left him with no alternative. He had always been prepared for that moment and was fortunate to have never had to pull the trigger of his weapon. He had gathered from the information he was provided from the killer that these men had been in operation for numerous years, and the list of victims likely went on for sometime.

He had no doubt they had made numerous enemies over the years and that any number of their connections could be responsible, but David had a feeling it was connected, but in a much different way. The fact they chose only to harm them and not their families told him they weren't dealing with a paid assassin who would not have cared if the family had witnessed the killing or if the families themselves had to be killed. No, this person was dispensing their sense of justice to only those they deemed guilty of whatever crime that would have the killer to want an eye for eye as they had stated in their message to him.

The only devastating occurrence he had ever heard story of in the community was the death of some officer and his family. The town had always been a quiet place to live where most of the people were friendly and kind. He couldn't recall the name on the case but thought he would take a look when he went back to his office. He did recall how the chief reacted when he mentioned it since it seemed to be the worst occurrence in the town's history. What intrigued his thoughts more was he thought he remembered it being an Irish name, but he couldn't recall for certain. He wasn't sure what sparked the thought in his mind, but he wanted to take a look to see if they might have had family incarcerated who may have been released recently and just had the opportunity. If the officer had been involved in the same activities, it is likely his family connections could possibly as well.

David was so close to being fully prepared to make the county-wide sweep, along with a couple of other locations; he felt he could begin to focus his attention back to trying to caste a profile of the killer that made sense to him. After all, it was connected with the current raid, and somewhere among them may be the killer, and if he could get an idea of what they might look like from the little film he had available from the hotel, he might be able to recognize them. He had requested Kevin have an expert take care of it, and the envelope he had given David earlier had the results, but Kevin did tell him it was poor quality, so the guy could only guess on some features. He thought it could be enough to give him a general visual to go by, and he would use what he could get.

Regardless of what the killer's intention or motive, they had broken the law, and David was bound to his duty as an enforcer of the law. He could not allow his opinion of the victims to influence his obligations to uphold the law. There was never a doubt he would do whatever the law states is dutiful, but something inside of him felt torn and he couldn't identify what it was. Something was telling him these men had committed a horrible crime and they were receiving their just rewards, if one believes in karma. Whoever killed these men had to have received special training to have pulled off what the killer had managed to.

From what he had seen of the killer in the video, it appeared to him they were small in stature, if they were indeed a man. It was the killer's movements that led him to believe they were female. He had seen men with feminine mannerisms and women with masculinity, but even with the killer trying to maneuver their steps to avoid being seen by the camera, they appeared to be more of the feminine nature. Regardless, there was a distinct difference in the walk of a male in comparison with a female, and David was going with it being a female. He believed this because the killer hadn't taunted him in their assistance with identifying locations they promised they would. Instead, they were polite and helpful and not condemning.

"Hell, even the strikes made by the pen on the map they provided shows feminine characteristics," David spoke out loud as he stepped down on to the pavement beneath his feet, turning briefly to confirm he had grabbed everything he wanted to take into his office with him before locking the Jeep doors and turning toward the building. He began humming the tune to the song "Windows" by Angel Olsen, which seemed so appropriate to reflect what he wished to say to the killer once they met as he made his way to his office.

David set everything down to one side of his desk which hadn't already been littered with files and paperwork and headed to the coffee machine down the hall. He was thankful to find a freshly brewed pot and filled his cup close to the rim before turning back to his office where he sat back in his chair and sipped at the cup of steaming brew before locating the file he had wanted to review, along with everything Kevin had been able to obtain for him.

David leafed through the file and came across some old photos of the officer and his deceased family. He stared at the black-and-white photos of the officer and his family. They were extremely attractive people with distinctive facial features and attractive builds. They appeared to be happy in the photos he viewed, and he felt in his gut the officer didn't appear to be the type of man who would do what he was accused of. There was a kindness in his eyes that David sensed was genuine.

He had always been such a good read of people and wasn't sure what it was, but it was almost as if he could read a person just by being around them for a brief time and observing them. It almost felt to him as if he had actually tapped into their minds and could see their thoughts. He felt he had always had a sense of awareness about him even as a young child. He was never quite able to fully understand whatever gave him the extra sense, but he had been thankful for having listened on more than one occasion.

Grabbing up the next stack of photos, David was interrupted with a call from one of the guys assisting with the investigation. He gave David his location and asked him to meet him and another special agent at that mark, and he warned David to bring a mask with him because he would need it to help with the smell. David placed the stack he still held in hand back into the file and closed it before grabbing his keys and cup of coffee and putting the coordinates provided him into his tracker and followed the directions it provided. He was surprised when it told him to follow the dirt road to the right because, from what he could see, there was no road to the right.

David stepped from the Jeep and walked to the edge of the woods and looked in more closely to see if he could see any signs of a previous road having been there. He was able to see that it did have an opening approximately fifteen feet wide that led back through, but new growth had begun to mask its existence. He climbed back into the Jeep and put it in low gear in case he hit some rocky areas and followed what he believed to be a road leading into the forest. He came to a small stream area but was able to easily pass through it and continued to follow the tracks made from previous vehicles. He could tell he was heading in the right direction still because the tracker showed the distance getting smaller and smaller now. He came to an area that appeared to have a turn around, and about fifty yards up the hill, he could see a small cabin. He stepped from his vehicle and made the rest of the way by foot.

"Did you bring something to cover your face?" he could hear one of the men yell down as he hiked the hill toward them.

"I have a mask with me," David explained before asking if it was really that bad to both men.

"You won't be able to get the smell from your nose, and trust me, you will never forget that smell," the other guy replied. "The dogs found it and won't even come farther than the tree line. Anyway, I think we found your chief."

"Why would you assume it's the chief if the body smells that bad? It has to be decomposing," David questioned, walking closer to the cabin. He was already able to pick up a putrid scent in the air. He placed the mask over his head before proceeding farther and found that it blocked the majority of the odor, but it was so intense it was able to find its way into the mask, causing him to hurry through with viewing what had been seen by the other two men. It was definitely the chief's uniform, which lay neatly folded nearby the body that was now infested with maggots that ate at the rotting flesh. He was able to take a couple of quick shots before nearly running for the door of the cabin so that he could take in a deep breath of air. He had regretted pulling the mask off even at a safe distance from the cabin because his clothing was saturated by the smell, and he felt he could now taste it in his mouth. He gagged momentarily before being able to pull himself together before the other two reached him.

"Would you say that's your missing chief?" one asked as he arrived next to David. "Sorry about that, but I tried to warn you."

"Based on what we saw, I would safely presume it is the chief, but we will need an autopsy to be sure," David advised before asking if they had called in a team to take care of the crime scene and was told they had but wanted him to see it first. He had no doubt it was the same killer. They had left their message which would need translated, but there was something so different about this one which struck David as odd. The killer had previously made their work displays, but this one they kept hidden away, as if it had a special purpose or message they weren't prepared to have found yet. He wanted Aislinn to take the photos of the crime scene, but there was no way he was going to expose her to that, so he did the best he could in what he took and hoped she could possibly enhance them and translate them for him, if she was available.

David thanked the guys for the call and told them he would be back later. His mind reeled as to whether he was able to get a clear view of the area and hadn't missed something important in his rush to get out of there. Clearly, from what he had seen from the killer's previous actions and public displays where the bodies would be found easily left him with the opinion that the chief wasn't supposed to be found until much later.

David's mind exploded in a million different directions now, causing him to perspire a little, so he cranked the air-conditioning on high and pressed the gas pedal harder. He was anxious to see what the message revealed in hopes it would give him the break he needed to identify them before they killed anyone else. He knew they would have a team to analyze the crime scene, but he wanted answers fast, and he knew Aislinn could decipher it within minutes. He thought for a moment how coincidental it was that she just happened to be in town after the first murder and incidentally knows the language and history. His thoughts ended with the idea she had been sent to help him. His views of Aislinn had been formed within their many encounters, and he felt she had one of the kindest hearts he had ever met. She had an innocence and awareness to her at the same time he found endearing. She was a well-studied individual with a brilliant mind and a zest for learning. He sensed there was a hidden layer to Aislinn he hadn't yet been able to figure out because she was private when it came to her personal life.

Most of what David knew about her, he found out by checking into her background. She had definitely traveled and spent many of her years abroad studying. David was impressed with her "never give up" attitude and courage. He was aware he had fallen in love with her but did what he could not to show it because he wanted her to want to stay of her own accord. He never wanted her to have any regrets, and he had heard her mention several times her future plans regarding her career. She had never mentioned wanting a family or children of her own although he could clearly see she would make a great mother. She was different than most women he had known, and he felt that may be what he found so intriguing about her. She didn't fit into any molds and wasn't afraid to be herself, and that impressed him. She was indeed a rare gem, and he hoped he had made a lasting impression on her as she had him.

He pulled in front of her cottage and noticed her car was gone, but he thought he would check to see if maybe she was there anyway. He knocked on the door and waited to see if he heard anyone inside, and when he was sure she wasn't there, he headed back to his Jeep and dialed her number. The phone rang several times before going to her voice mail; he hesitated before leaving her a message, asking her to call him back as soon as she was available. He thought he would drive through town to see if maybe she had run errands or was doing more research at the library. He really wanted to find out what the message from the killer said and was anxious to get in touch with her. He grew a little discouraged when he wasn't able to find her around town and resisted dialing her phone again. He knew there was no way she could have already heard about the chief since he was the only person notified, so he had no worries she would have found her way to the most recent crime scene. He agreed he would give her more time before trying her phone once more, so he headed back to his office and loaded the photos he had taken of the scene onto his computer to see if he could find a translation that made sense to him. He typed in as best he could to make out each letter written in the blood of the victim that the killer had meticulously scribed. It was as simple as telling him they are close to winning the war. What was it about those words that were so special that they wouldn't have made this killing as obvious as the others? he wondered. The thought came blasting into his mind as if it had been fired into his brain like a bullet. David recalled how the chief's uniform had been neatly folded precisely as an officer folds them, and he realized the killer had to be a cop or related to one. That was the message the killer wanted sent to him; he knew it had to be. He had a feeling they had a high regard for what the uniform represented, but not the officer who donned it.

David stood and stretched for a moment before going to get a cup of coffee. He thought he would take the opportunity to try to reach Aislinn again and seemed disappointed that it had gone straight to her voice mail once more. David almost didn't leave a message but decided he should tell her he already took care of what he had needed earlier and thanked her anyway. He hung up the phone so that he didn't ramble on and, for the first time, wondered if maybe she wasn't already seeing someone else and he was interrupting their time together. The mere thought of her possibly caring for another man made him feel as if he had been punched in the gut. *Could it be that the perfect woman for me is taken?* he thought to himself. The impossibility of the question seemed more likely than her being in a relationship, he argued, as he continued to think of the many reasons he believed her to be single.

"Dear Lord," David said out loud, "this woman has absolutely captivated my heart, and I don't know if I can find a cure for that."

David poured his cup of coffee and turned to head back to his office. He thought he might take a look at more of the file he had been going through before he was called out to the crime scene. He thought there was a possibility they had records of others who may have been involved, and it could give him some help with potential motive for murder and a suspect.

CHAPTER 24

She lurked outside of the tavern along the edge of the parking lot where the trees cast a dark shadow over the dim parking lot lights close to the building. She could see his truck parked in the back, and she hunkered down close to the tree base and watched for any signs of movement.

It had started to sprinkle, but she would have to tough it out. This would be her last opportunity to get Moran alone before the detective made his raid. The stranger figured the detective had already connected Moran to the local meth lab ring, and there was no way she was going to allow him to make it to a trial. He was going to pay for his part as the others did. He was the last piece to finish the puzzle that would allow her to move forward in her life and forget everything that had taken up nearly the majority of her life, except the memories she had of her family. She was ready to see what was out there in the world beyond her years of preparation for these past couple of months of fulfilling what she had come to do.

She heard the sound of a door opening, and she adjusted her eyes and saw that it was Moran leaving through the back door. She jumped to her feet and looked around the parking lot before approaching him near his truck.

"Excuse me, sir," she interrupted his gait. "I was hoping you might be able to help me out. I just got into town here, and I wasn't prepared for this rain."

"Get to the point, Missy," he ordered, beginning to step toward his truck again.

"Well, sir, to be honest with you, I don't have any money and I was hoping that I could catch a ride with you to get out of this rain.

I thought you looked like a nice guy and all," she replied, putting her head down in embarrassment and brushing the tip of her shoe back and forth across the pavement to deflect his attention from her face.

"What do I look like?" he mumbled, opening the door of his truck and trying to position himself to climb up to the seat.

"Please, sir," she pleaded, hoping to not have to pull her gun now. "I don't have any family and no one I can turn to. I am just asking for food. That's all."

"No family, huh?" he grumbled, sitting himself behind the wheel of the truck. "Oh hell, get in."

"Thank you, sir," she replied, trying to reflect gratitude and desperation. "You won't regret this."

"No, but you will," he muttered under his breath as she walked around the back of the truck to climb in the passenger seat.

"I can't thank you enough for your generosity," she jabbed on incessantly. "It has been a couple of days since I have had a good meal. What sounds good to you?"

"Take your pick. I have already eaten," he replied, smirking at her upcoming circumstances.

"Oh my god, I could go for some of that Arby's right over there!" she exclaimed with excitement as he drove down the street. "You don't know what you are missing right here, my friend."

He handed her twenty dollars and told her to go inside and get her food, and he would wait in the truck for her and give her a ride. He placed a call to one of his partners and told them he might have a present for them they hadn't planned on.

The stranger exited the truck and walked into the restaurant and tried to decide what she could eat that would keep her story believable. She ordered and made her way back to the truck, sipping at the milkshake on her way. She climbed back in the passenger seat and reached in her jacket pocket to retrieve his change. She reached out to hand it to him, and he told her to go ahead and keep it in case she needed something the next day.

He looked around before throwing the truck in reverse and barked the tires when he put it in drive. He asked her if she liked a little excitement, of which she assured him she did. He told her he wanted to take her for a ride and have a little fun together before he would take her to a motel to get her a room.

There was no question in her mind where he intended to take her, and that was exactly where she didn't want to go. She knew they would be casing the area, and she did not want any of the special agents to have an opportunity to possibly catch her on film. She would let him drive out a distance where she didn't feel she had to worry about traffic before pulling out her gun and telling him where he was going to go. She nibbled at the sandwich as she scooted down in the seat to avoid any oncoming lights reflecting her face for someone to recognize. She would give him an occasional sideways glance so she could check to see if he was carrying. She hadn't been able to properly assess his truck yet, but she didn't think he had any guns on his person. She allowed her eyes to scan the interior of his truck, and unless he had a pistol in the glove compartment, it appeared to be clean. She would remain alert in case he did have one she had missed; that way she would have the upper hand still.

"So you don't have any kinfolk? Is that right?" Moran inquired as he continued the irritating sucking noise he made through his teeth with his tongue. "What if you were to come up missing? There wouldn't be anyone to miss you."

"It's highly unlikely that I will come up missing," she replied, sitting back with confidence against the truck's seat, smiling to reflect her lack of fear.

"I mean, a pretty little girl like you," he began, looking over at her with an intimidating glare, "there are lots of fellas out there who would love a chance to get in those pants."

"They should worry more about what would happen to them if they tried, and I didn't like what they were doing," she warned, the smile faded from her face and a look of absolution came over it.

"What's a tiny little thing like you going to do?" he asked, moving his free hand toward her leg and stopping inches from her. "If a man wants you, he is going to have you."

"I wish him the best of luck then," she declared, continuing to watch the road ahead since they were getting close to where she saw them keeping the others.

"Aren't you a lot of fun," he mocked, pulling his hand back to the wheel and watching the road more closely.

She waited until she could feel the truck decelerate and come close to the turn before uncovering the gun beneath her jacket aimed directly at him and ordered him to keep going down the road and to follow her instructions.

Moran straightened the wheel and picked up speed after assessing his situation. He waited several minutes before asking her any questions and followed her instructions to remain silent until she was ready to speak.

Other than an occasional barking of orders, she remained silent and stared at him as though if she were to blink, he would disappear. This was the last of the trash to be taken out, and she didn't want to make any mistakes. He was a soulless man, and she had no doubts about that, so she guarded herself against any defense he could still maneuver. She could see his mind working through the alcohol, and he had become sober, causing her to be more alert and having a desire to put even more space between them. It was a matter of minutes until they reached the turn to the back side of the woods surrounding her father's cabin. She would have to finish him there since it was outside of the county lines, and she wouldn't have any concerns about being seen by any of the agents. It was a risky trail in the dark with steep drops up to sixty feet if you aren't paying attention to your step. The rain hadn't let up, and that would make parts of the trail slick, but she had to push on, or she may not get another opportunity for years. She was confident he would get life with a possibility of parole many years down the road, and she didn't feel it would be fair to the taxpayer to house and feed someone she considered less than an animal, who had destroyed numerous innocent lives and dashed hundreds of dreams. She had him pull down the narrow path approximately seventy-five yards from the tree line and ordered him to get out of the truck.

"It seems to me that you have the intention of killing me if I do listen to you, so why don't you just go ahead and get it over with?" He resisted, staying seated with both hands on the steering wheel.

"Maybe, but then again maybe not," she voiced nonchalantly. "I can guarantee you that if you don't, you will force me to splatter your brains all over this fine leather seat of your truck. I was hoping we could take a walk and have a chat along the way."

"Can't we do that here where we are dry and warm?" he asked, reaching his hand down along the outside of his seat.

"Put your hand back up on the wheel," she ordered, putting the tip of the gun hard against his temple.

Moran turned his head to face her, ignoring the gun pressing against his face but complying with her request as he could see in her eyes she meant what she said.

"Now get out and step away from the vehicle, but keep your arms up," she ordered again as she scooted across the seat and into the driver's, stepping down gently behind him and allowing him a three-foot distance in front of her. "Follow that path right there."

Moran took a few steps in the direction she pointed but complained about not being able to see anything in front of him. He requested she allow him to get a flashlight from his tool box so he could light the way for them. She asked him where it was located and took the key from him to unlock it herself. She had been smart in doing so because he had a revolver in the top shelf of the box. She congratulated him for trying and threw the flashlight in his direction and told him to pick it up. He did as she ordered and started up the path she had originally directed him.

The stranger was cursing beneath her breath for having worn sneakers and not boots as she followed him up the hill, but she hadn't anticipated the rain, and it was falling harder now. She could see little of the path because his body covered most of the light that would have reflected around the flashlight. The forest was now pitch-black around them with the exception of the light given off by the flashlight. She would occasionally hear a twig snap off in the distance and chalked it up to deer.

"So what's this all about?" Moran called back to her over the wind and rain. "What did I do to wrong you?"

"I will cut to the chase since I am not really in the mood to talk," she began, wiping the rain from her face as it pounded against it, making it difficult to speak. "Do you remember the O'Conner family?"

Moran froze on the path and turned to face her with a look she had seen from some of the townsfolk she had asked. She could see the color drain from his face as he stood there with a dumbfounded look on his face.

"I asked you a question!" she yelled over the wind. "Do you remember them?"

"Why do you ask?" he came back with a question, standing there, awaiting her reply.

She moved closer to him and screamed at him to look at her face, and she lifted her head proudly up at him and stared at him in the face and watched as the look of fear washed over his face.

"You killed the others, didn't you?" he asked after regaining his composure.

"Would it make you feel better or worse if I were to say yes?" she asked with an amused grin on her face.

"What's any of that have to do with you?" he asked, turning to walk again as she had requested. "It isn't like you were there. I mean what are you, a sister or cousin?"

"I am that twelve-year-old child you thought you had killed!" she screamed above the crashing thunder. "The little girl you and your friends replaced the body of because mine had somehow disappeared from those of my parents and my brother. Is it making any sense to you now?"

"Can't we just talk about this?" he pleaded, walking carefully up the hill so as not to trip over the tree roots lodged in the dirt like stairsteps. He made use of them to keep his footing on the slick mud that was forming on the ground.

"We are talking, Mr. Moran," she mocked, watching her step closely. "What else would you call it?"

Moran hadn't personally seen the remains of his fellow comrades, but he had heard the stories from a couple of the officers he served with before retiring on disability, and he had no doubt what her plan was for him also. He gave up trying to communicate with her and decided he would try to flee his first chance. He figured if he could get away soon, he would have no problem finding his way back to where his truck was parked.

"So are you and that reporter chick friends?" Moran asked, pausing to catch his air briefly. "You know, the one who came to my house and spoke with my wife?"

"No, but I have to give that girl credit." The stranger smiled a rue grin, trying to keep her balance on the slippery path. The dampness made the tree roots and rocks slick and the sandy soil loose, making the climb more difficult. "She is certainly on top of things. Much smarter than your junkie friends you hire. Those boys didn't know what to do with themselves when I interrupted your delivery."

Moran stopped on the trail again, breathless and confused by her statement, since he hadn't yet heard the news about the two men who had been arrested and the kids rescued they had testifying for the state. The stranger was pleased to share what she knew of the incident with Moran and watched as he realized his world was about to come to an end one way or another.

She motioned for him to continue and followed as she had the entire trail. She could tell they were getting fairly close to the cabin because they had nearly reached the top of the ridge that led down to the sloping hills that would follow and the cabin set on the top just as the two separated.

Moran had no idea his two men had been caught; had he known, he wouldn't have wasted any more time locating new victims for their sex slave trade, and she was a little older than they usually like, but he figured they could pass her off as almost eighteen. Had he been paying closer attention, he would have already taken the cash he had hidden over the years and found a safe place where he could hide out until he felt enough time had passed. He had enough money to keep him comfortable for the rest of his life. He could still do it, he thought to himself, if he could find the right moment to disarm his current abductor and get rid of that nosy reporter along with her.

They walked another half mile, and both were drenched from the relentless raindrops that fell in torrents from the sky. The leaves on the trees all seemed to look downward from the weight of the waterdrops. They could smell the soil and remnants of last years' decomposing limbs and leaves in the warm moist air. They were getting ready to walk around tree that left little room for them along the edge close to a deep ravine. She had seen it as he shown the light ahead of them, and as she nearly reached the corner of the tree, everything went completely dark. The flashlight had disappeared, and as she went to swipe the rain-drenched hair from her face, the light hit her in the face, along with the large end of the flashlight. She nearly caught her balance, but the weight of his body against hers sent her over the edge of the path and tumbling down the edge of the stonewall. She reached out for anything she could grab in hopes of slowing her fall, but it was too late; her body smashed against the trunk of a tree growing from the side of the ledge and slammed her against the stonewall, knocking her unconscious. She slid several more feet in a tangled heap onto a rock ledge about a foot and half wide. Moran carefully leaned over the edge and shined the light down to see if he could see where she landed. He was satisfied as he watched through the dim light, her lifeless body twisted and contorted in a crumpled heap on the ledge.

"Whoa," he said, stepping back from the edge when he saw the distance of the drop. "I doubt you survived that, you little bitch, but I'll be back to make sure after I catch up with your little friend."

He looked around to see if he could locate the gun in case she dropped it before falling but then figured it would be of no need to him now. He slowly turned and worked his way back down the steep incline they had just come up and looked for any signs of their tracks on the way back. Some were still evident, but others had washed away with all the rain. He tried to snap limbs to mark the trail, for when he came back to deal with her body, he could locate her without too much trouble. He hoped she would still be alive so he could finish her off the way he wanted—with as much pain as possible. It took him nearly forty-five minutes to find his way back to his truck, and when he climbed inside, he let out a bellow of anger so loud it could be heard over the clapping thunder and pounding rain. He was furious she had the audacity to come back and make an attempt to ruin everything he had worked hard to keep running for so many years.

A couple of the others had opted out a few years earlier, but Moran had kept business going at the same rate without them. He felt they had gone soft, so it was high time they walk away in his opinion. He reached into the back seat of the truck and found a towel he could use to wipe some of the rain and mud from his face and hands where he had slipped and fallen a few times on his way back. He wasn't worried about the interior of his truck right now because he doubted he would be around to drive it. He would have to find another vehicle for now if he was going to have any chance of making it out of the next couple of counties. A sly smile covered his face as he thought about the reporter's car since she wouldn't need it very soon as dead people don't drive. He wouldn't draw attention in her car because no one would suspect anything, and it would take them some time to locate her body once he was finished with her.

Moran pulled slowly down his street and looked around to see if he noticed any suspicious cars or people around. He noticed nothing out of the ordinary, so he pulled into the drive and ran to the house and quickly went inside. His wife jumped from the sofa and greeted him, but he walked past her and went downstairs where she called to him from the top of the stairs.

"I am in a hurry right now, but I need you to listen to me and pack the things I tell you to." Moran called out the items to his wife from down the stairs, and on his way back up after having stripped his clothes from earlier, he told her, "We are going on a trip. Take what you want only because we won't be returning. I don't have time for your questions, so don't start with any."

Mrs. Moran remained standing by the stairs with her arms crossed in front of her and stared at him like she hadn't heard anything he had just said to her.

"Well, go on and do what I told you to do, woman," Moran ordered again, still rushing around, gathering strange things together that made no sense to her.

"What have you done?" She looked at him with dead eyes. "I knew something wasn't right when that family died. It has something to do with their deaths, doesn't it?"

He stopped cold in his tracks and turned to look at his wife with dark eyes she'd seen on more than one occasion but no longer feared them. She felt she had died long ago but remained alive enough for their children to be happy, productive people. He had been physically aggressive with her on several occasions, but he had never raised a hand to their children. She often believed it was stress from his job, but when he retired with disability, he wasn't around any more than before retiring, and he hadn't shared with her his activities, but she didn't mind; she went on living for their children and helping in the community where she could.

"Mind your own business and do what you are told," he demanded as he tossed each of the items in a bag and began putting on his rain gear. "I'll be back in the morning and you had better be ready."

Moran stormed out the door and tossed the bag on the front seat of the truck completely unaware that his wife stood in the same spot she had been when he barked his orders. He had no idea that she had other plans, and they had nothing to do with leaving with him. It wouldn't have mattered to him at the time because his thoughts were on returning to where he had shoved the stranger from the cliffside and to find the cabin that belonged to her father so that he could take the reporter there to make it appear that the killer had also murdered her. That would eliminate anyone who may have figured out or been associated with the killer, and he would be the only remaining witness to that long ago day's events. The more he thought about how careless his dead partners had been, the angrier he became. He was going to finish the story once and for all himself. If they caught up with him for being involved with the drugs and other activities in the event one of his current partners turned state evidence against him, his time spent would be minimal compared to how things would go if they discovered his involvement in the murders.

Nearing the spot where they pulled off, he checked to see if there were any vehicles in the area before making the turn and pulling to the spot she had made him stop earlier. He grabbed the bag from the seat and pulled his rain hat over his head and made the trek back up the path to the spot where he had shoved her. He shined the light over the edge but was unable to get a good view of where he had seen her body fall earlier. He needed to find another way down so that he could scan the area for any traces of her. He knew she had to have sustained serious injuries from having fallen so far. There was no way she couldn't have broken several bones if she even survived it. He made his way around the ledge once more and followed what appeared to be a path, and lo and behold, he nearly stumbled right over the cabin.

"You always were a smart son of a bitch." Moran bellowed a delighted gut laugh as he looked around with the flashlight and allowed himself to be impressed with the stranger's father's ingenious location for the cabin. "I see why we weren't able to find it before now. It's a damn shame you had to go and blow it. We really could have used a guy like you."

He made his way down the path that led down into the ravine where he could look around to see if he could find her. He knew she had to be somewhere in this area, and he would find her.

"You had better pray I find you dead, you little bitch!" Moran yelled out over the rain as he continued his search of the area. He was able to see from below where she had fallen, and he found pieces of a shirt that had been torn, obviously to make a tourniquet. "So you are alive, and that means I am going to get to have some more fun."

CHAPTER 25

David tried again to reach Aislinn, but still she did not respond to his call. He had left several messages and was certain she would have returned at least one of his calls, if to say nothing more than she was busy and unable to take his call. He was struggling to keep his attention on the plan as the raids were about to begin. They had everyone in place and ready to move once the signal was given. He had hoped for the rain to stop, but it was actually to their advantage since it muffled any noise they could accidentally make, ruining their element of surprise.

This was, by far, the largest bust to ever take place within the entire area. They had discovered connections all along the route between Clare and Philadelphia, which is why it made it difficult for law enforcement to locate the missing people as they are moved from one location to the next. They try to remove them as far away from their familiar surroundings so they are completely dependent upon them and do as they say. David was repulsed that a man could have a sexual relationship with a woman he did not know or love for that matter, let alone a young girl. He struggled to find any reasoning behind such behavior and couldn't come up with a plausible excuse. In his opinion, men who behave in such an offensive manner are not men but mere brainless bodies walking around and doing more harm than good. He questioned what illness a man has who finds it a turn on to force a woman to have sex when she is an unwilling participant and how is that a challenge when men are physically stronger than a woman. These were the type of men he had no use for and felt they needed their brains rewired because they weren't normal.

David had allowed his frustration for these types to distract him, and he didn't see the branch dangling in front him being blown about by the wind until a sharp edge had caught him on the cheek just below his left eye. He reached his hand up, and when he brought it back, he could see the red-stained fingers from the blood that dripped down his cheek from the gash. His frustration built because he had been making his way back to the other men after going to his vehicle to avoid the rain so that he could try to reach Aislinn and was still unable. His frustration turned to concern as he thought about how stubborn she could be, and his mind raced at the endless possibilities. He was completely aware of the extent these people would go to keep their operation running since it was such a lucrative business.

Aislinn would impose a major threat to their establishment, and they wouldn't hesitate to kill her or worse. This is what he found more exasperating than her not recognizing her own beauty. She had no idea how her smile lit up a room, and her laughter was some of the sweetest music he had ever heard, but she had this uncanny way of discovering dangerous situations and putting herself in them. Living with her would be great, but with her reckless disregard for her own safety, he wondered how he would live without her. He knew she would risk her life to expose such an atrocity as this and that this would not be her last story. He wished he could think of something magical to say that would make her want to stay and give up her career, but he figured he didn't have much excitement to offer that would make it even tempting for her.

"It looks like we'll be ready to move in soon, Detective," one of the officers interrupted his thoughts. "I just got a report that almost everyone is in position and ready to move."

"Thank you for that update," David replied, trying to clear his mind and get focused to move in as he joined them under the tarp they had put up to shield them from the heavy rain and waited for word to proceed forward with executing the operation.

CHAPTER 26

Aislinn's eyes opened with a start, and she felt that she was suffocating, unaware of the hand that covered her mouth and nose until she had gained full consciousness. Her instincts kicked in, and she began to claw at her assailant and kick and thrash, trying to escape his grasp, but his hold was too tight and left her no room to move.

"Now, now." She heard the deep masculine voice in a threatening tone rather than the pretentious, innocent, soothing sound it was meant to portray. "Do as I say and you might just make it out of this alive."

"What do you want?" Aislinn asked calmly, belying the throb going on in her heart once he had slowly released his hand from her mouth.

"Ah, ah, ah, you naughty girl," he taunted, forcing her head away from him once more. "No peeking and I think we both know why I am here."

"I honestly have no idea why a strange man is in my bedroom in the middle of the night holding a gun to the middle of my back and asking me to play a guessing game after rudely awaking me," Aislinn retaliated, expecting the blow that followed shortly after her last word escaped her lips.

"Don't try to be cute with me and think that your looks are going to spare you," he mocked in her face. "I have fucked many beautiful girls. Some begged for it and some just begged. I can't wait to see what you will do, but first we have someplace we need to visit. A special little hideaway where we can find your friend."

"What friend is that?" Aislinn asked, praying that he was not referring to David as she took another blow to her back from the butt of the gun. He took his free hand and shoved her face down into the pillow and drew her behind in the air as he pressed his body against her and felt her left breast with his free hand. He began to pant as he rubbed himself against her, using his free hand to run it all over her body, before abruptly pulling away and handing her the robe he found next to the bed.

"Put it on and let's go," he demanded, taking a few steps away, allowing her space to cover herself with her robe and enough distance in case she tried to disarm him.

"Where are we going, Mr. Moran?" she asked, letting him know she knew who he was as she made her way from the bedroom.

"I see your memory has returned," he replied with a sly, hateful grin on his face, following her into the next room and informing her they would be taking her car since the police would be looking for his.

Aislinn could clearly see the confused look that came across Moran's face as he saw her for the first time in the light.

"You act as if you are seeing a ghost, Mr. Moran," Aislinn explained in response to the pallor that swept over his face, giving him the appearance of being a ghost himself.

"This can't be," Moran stuttered, clearly unable to recover from his shock. "Who are you, and how did you do that?"

"Do what?" she inquired, raising one eyebrow to reflect her confusion.

"Shut up!" he screamed, pointing the gun at her wildly as he stood there shaking his head. "You just shut up and do what I tell you."

"Okay, I am doing everything you say," Aislinn continued in a calm tone, aware of his confusion.

"This time I am going to cut your fucking heart out and let's see if you come back then, you bitch!" he screamed, appearing like a madman as he shoved her toward the door after demanding the keys to her car. When she didn't respond fast enough for his liking, he grabbed her by her hair and jerked her against him, shoving the gun in her ribs.

Aislinn wanted to scream out from the pain he caused her, but she restrained and remained calm, and in doing so, she could feel his grasp on her hair begin to release, and she was able to straighten her posture once again. She quickly glided her way to where she kept her purse, and rather than reach inside, she handed her purse to him and told him where to find them so that he would not shoot her, thinking she was trying to go for a weapon.

Moran ripped the purse from her extended hand and reached into the outer pocket as she had advised and located the car remote. He gestured for her to move toward the door, and she did as he advised. She glanced around for anything she might be able to use to disarm him but failed to see anything substantial enough to guarantee her gaining the upper hand. She doubted she would come close to being able to access her own weapon, so she complied and decided she would come up with another solution. She stepped to the side as she watched Moran fumble with the door lock, and finally after several seconds, he jerked it open and motioned for her to exit.

"Can I get my raincoat?" she asked, still dressed only in her robe. "I could also use my rain boots."

"I suppose I could allow you that since I have no plan of carrying you," he mocked as he followed her back into her bedroom. "Don't worry that pretty little head though. I will be keeping you warm later."

Aislinn cringed at the thought of him even touching her as he had earlier, and she could feel her muscles tense and harden, but again she kept her calm and slid her feet into the boots and covered herself with her raincoat before heading outside to her car. He directed her in a loud voice so that she could hear him over the rain. He was having her drive, which ruined her chance of being able to exit the car at a convenient moment and have even the slightest opportunity to escape unharmed. She climbed into the driver's seat as he fell into the passenger's seat and flopped his muddy boots against the doorframe as he positioned himself in the seat.

"Nice car," he complimented as he continued looking around. "This should do me real nice. Of course, I will have it cleaned up all nice like you keep it."

Aislinn ignored his comment and awaited his instructions, her mind reeled with possibilities but none felt safe enough, so she pressed the Start button and waited for him to tell her where to drive. A flashing green light in the side door reminded her she had left her phone there earlier and had forgotten. If she could press the screen without it lighting up too much, she might be able to get a call out to whoever the last caller was. She decided she would wait until they were in a more lit area so it wouldn't appear as bright and take her chance then. She put the car in Drive and followed the direction he requested. It didn't matter which direction they took; they would come to a lit area where she would distract him long enough to place the call and hope that whoever was on the other end would be able to hear without being heard. She would hit the volume on her radio if she had to and make it appear to be an accident. This might be her only hope of getting help because her situation seemed to be getting bleaker each passing moment. She slowed the car as they approached a traffic light, and she hoped to catch it red so that she could press Call once the light turned green and the screen light would be less noticeable. She nearly smiled as she saw the light change from yellow to red, and she casually placed her left arm down and waited the changing of the light, and as soon as it flickered to green, she pressed her phone and hit the Return Call button without glancing in the direction of the phone. She slightly altered the volume of the stereo from the steering column to prevent him from hearing the slight tone of the ring coming from her phone. Her hands became clammy and damp on the steering wheel from the rush of adrenaline that flooded through her veins.

"You have made your intentions clear, but may I ask where we are going?" Aislinn inquired, hoping he would provide whoever it was on the other end of the phone some details as to where they might be going.

"Don't pretend like you aren't familiar with that quaint little cabin in the woods where you intended to try to kill me like you and your friend did the others," he warned, glaring at her with hatred in his eyes. "I just haven't figured out what part you play yet, but I can guarantee you by the time I finish with you, you'll be singing your heart out."

"I am not sure what you think I can provide you regarding the killer," she began in her response. "I have been waiting to meet them myself. I do, however, have questions regarding the death of one of your fellow officers and his family. That's all I came to discuss."

Moran belted out a sadistic laugh and slapped his hand on his knee as though he were actually finding amusement in her reply. Aislinn knew he was toying with her when he looked her in the eyes, and she saw how black they were around the pupil. The warning signs flashed bright in her head, and she knew that she had been correct in believing there was much more to their deaths than she had suspected.

"Did Abigail tell you what we did to her?" he asked, his voice becoming raspy as he reached over with his hand and began stroking a lock of her hair.

"How could she when she's dead?" Aislinn asked, trying not to acknowledge his attention. "You are referring to the child, aren't you?"

"You and I both know that she's not dead," he taunted, moving his hand along the opening to her robe and sliding his hand inside it. He took the nipple of her breast between his thumb and index finger and began to squeeze it hard until Aislinn brought her right arm up and jerked the opposite direction away from him. He grabbed her hair from the side and jerked her head around roughly but released her quickly since she was still driving the car. "I am going to enjoy fucking you the same way I did her."

Aislinn's stomach began churning as the image of him forcing himself on that child sickened her beyond her ability to maintain her composure. She could feel the bile rising, so she quickly hit the window release and leaned her head out the window to spit it up. She could hear his evil laughter over the wind blowing against her face as she held her head out the window. Wiping the rain from her face, she turned to look at him, and the contempt she had for him reflected.

"I want you to fight," he taunted, leaning in closer to her. "I love it when they fight. She fought all the way up to the end, you know, before she passed out from all the bleeding. Damn tight little virgin she was. I was the first to fuck her, and I will never forget how it felt."

Aislinn screamed inside from his words, and at that moment, she herself wanted to kill him. The rage inside her almost drove her to kill herself to ensure he was dead as she contemplated speeding up and driving the car into a tree, but there was no guarantee he would die, so she continued to drive along the instructed route.

"What's this?" Moran asked, appearing to be nervous and causing Aislinn to look in her rearview mirror to see the flashing lights coming from behind her car at a high rate of speed. She prayed it was David who had found her, but the cars didn't slow down when she pulled off the side of the road slowly, listening to Moran threaten her if she attempted to warn the officers as their cars raced past them.

Aislinn pulled the car back onto the road and continued in the same direction of the lights that flashed in front of them. A couple of miles up the road on the county line, she could see the officers had pulled over and appeared to be preparing for a roadblock. She continued to hope they would pull her car over, but they only waved her through as she slowed her speed to pass around them. She knew they got a good look at her and Moran, but they had no reason to stop them yet because the message was still recording, and he wouldn't be able to retrieve it until she ended the call. She wanted to give him as much detail as possible so that he could locate her and feared ending it too soon, so she left it going and hoped he was able to hear Moran's orders for her to take a right onto a dirt lane a couple of miles from the county line.

"I don't know if my car can make it on this trail," Aislinn warned Moran as she pulled slowly onto the side of the road where he had instructed her to turn. "I don't think my tires can make it through the mud. We will get stuck."

"Just drive slow," he ordered, looking around to see if he saw any headlights from either direction.

Aislinn hesitated before giving the car too much gas, causing it to spin from side to side, leaving tracks along the side of the road that could be seen by passersby. She aligned the tires over the ruts which appeared to have been made recently, but by a larger vehicle, to prevent the bottom of her car scraping and potentially getting hung up. She kept the car in low gear and followed the tracks that had been left by what she presumed had been Moran's truck. She was going slower than Moran would have liked, but he knew he could wait her out, and this gave him an opportunity to touch those magnificent breasts of hers without worrying about anyone seeing. It was as if she could sense what his thoughts were and hit the gas a little harder, throwing him against the seat unexpectedly, nearly causing him to lose control of the gun. He laughed out loud in recognition of her move and told her he could wait as he went on to tell her the things he planned to do to her once they made it back to the cabin while she thought of ways she might still possibly escape. She had considered jumping from the car and running, but she knew that with all of the rain the mud would slow her and she definitely wasn't fast enough to outrun a bullet. Her mind continued to race with ideas, but none of them seemed plausible once she reconsidered them.

"Which way does it go?" Aislinn asked, unclear which direction the tracks took after about twenty feet in front of her.

"We're at the end of the road," Moran explained. "I am afraid we will have to take a little hike, but that should only take about twenty minutes up the hill right there to your left unless you wish to run and make it less. I know how much you want this big dick. I'm sure your friend told you how big it is."

Aislinn ignored his taunts and proceeded to exit the car, and while doing so, she hit End on the call and moved slowly until the phone light went off. She stood beside the car and waited for Moran to make his way around to where she stood. He handed her a flashlight and pushed her in the direction of the hill and followed about three feet behind since he had become more familiar with the path. Aislinn slipped several times from the mud and steady rain but was able to regain her balance and continue. She followed what was left of the earlier footprints that were still somewhat evident, taking her time to provide whoever was on the phone a chance to get the call and take action. Any delays she could take advantage of, she did her best until she could tell Moran was catching on.

"You'll want to be careful up here," Moran warned her as she started her ascent upward until she almost reached the tree. "This is where your friend died. She fell standing almost right where you are with a little help from me, of course. Take a look over the edge, but you better make sure you don't slip."

Aislinn ran the light over the edge and could see that it was quite a drop to the bottom although the light didn't reach all the way to the end. She stepped back from the edge and reached out for the tree for stability, leaning there briefly until Moran reached her and urged her to move around the tree and farther up the incline. When she reached the top, she could see the ground level out again and was able to catch a faint smell of fire smoke in the air but saw no light other than what projected from the flashlight she carried. She followed the path which seemed to follow alongside a deep ravine to her right.

The ground seemed to stay fairly level, and the smell of the smoke became stronger as it laid low to the ground from the heavy rain. She could tell they were getting closer, and her mind raced with a million ideas at once with each step she took. She knew that unless someone knew where to look or stumbled onto the private property accidentally, they would have a very difficult time trying to find the location. The cabin was so well hidden behind a drove of pines with a large rock cliffside running behind it, making it impossible to see it from land or air. She had a sick feeling that her survival would depend solely on her now, and she wasn't dealing with a normal human being.

In her opinion, Moran was one of those soulless people, lacking in human compassion and believing himself to be a god. From what she had seen from him, he was of the opinion that anything not directly related to him was unworthy and deemed as nothing but mere instruments for his financial gain and pleasure, but when they no longer served either, they were discarded like garbage. People like Moran who have high regard for themselves and believe themselves to be entitled to certain things that others shouldn't be were the largest factor in affecting the remainder of society, but society as a whole had fallen asleep, at least that's how she viewed it. She felt that people never really learn from history or past personal experiences but keep falling back into their false sense of security and putting on their blinders, believing they aren't accountable for the errors of their leaders or those they allow as role models for the future generations.

Her thoughts were interrupted by the firm shove she received in the middle of her back from Moran that caused her to lose her footing and fall face-first into the muddy ground. The tiny rocks and limbs scratched against her skin, causing a scrape along her cheek and her upper shoulder. He picked her up by her hair and continued shoving her in the direction of the cabin. Aislinn knew she would have to take any opportunity presented to overcome him, if she had any chance of surviving the situation.

"It looks like we have arrived," Moran mocked, shoving her up the steps toward the cabin door. "Welcome to paradise. I hope you enjoy your stay."

Aislinn nearly stumbled over the threshold from the grasp Moran had on her hair that barely allowed her toes to reach the ground. He released her hair and shoved her toward the sofa where he ordered her to remain. She sat there soaked and breathing hard from the hike, not at all concerned about the damage occurring to the furniture. She could feel the heat from the fire, and it felt good to her chilled soaked body. Droplets of water continued to drip from the ends of her hair that was matted against her forehead, scalp, and back from the rain. Moran bent to retrieve another log from the pile to feed the fire before turning his attention back to Aislinn. He walked directly toward her, and when he reached her, he took her by the back of her head and shoved her face into his groin and rubbed hard against her, causing the scrapes on her cheek to bleed again. She tried twisting her head away, so he shoved her back against the sofa and slapped her hard across her face.

"You don't have to do this," Aislinn pleaded but was stifled with another slap across her mouth, busting her lower lip.

"Stand up," Moran ordered, grabbing her by the hair and pulling her up. "Now take the jacket and robe off."

Aislinn stood there and refused to do as he asked even after he punched her in the ribs several times with his fist and the butt of the gun; she remained noncompliant and refused to make it easy for him. She resisted all his attempts to remove her jacket and robe one handed, for he was unwilling to lay the gun down, so he crushed the butt of it against her left temple, rendering her unconscious.

Moran allowed her body to fall in a crumpled heap on the sofa and went about removing her attire and tossing it near the fireplace.

He laid her naked body out on the sofa and removed each of her boots, pitching them in the direction of her other belongings. He stood back and admired her beauty, and he could feel himself getting hard with the anticipation of feeling her. He bent over her and ran the tips of his fingers across her abdomen and up to her breasts, circling each nipple, sucking in his breath as he touched each one. Slowly, he rose and stepped back to retrieve the bag he had carried with him; reaching inside, he pulled out the strand of rope and began wrapping it several times around each of her wrists and cutting it off and tying the ends together.

Satisfied, he stood and took the remaining rope, made a noose on one end, and slung it over one of the rafters running across the room and secured it. He walked back to where she still lay unconscious and bent to lift her body. She was light to him as he placed her over his shoulder and then lowered her down the front of him as he prepared to tie the rope between the ropes securing her wrists. He pressed himself against her as he lowered her slowly down his front, pressing his erection against her. He reached around and unfastened his pants, rubbing his erection against her inner thighs while taking one of her breasts in his mouth. He wanted to enter her, but he wanted her to be awake so that he could watch her face as he pressed himself deep inside of her. Taking her by the arms, he pulled the rope through and began lifting her until her arms were over her head and her feet were touching the floor. He bent to place her feet together so that he could secure them with the remaining rope, and as he bent, he placed his tongue at the nape of her neck and ran it down the front of her until he reached her thighs where he lingered, licking at her roughly before pulling her legs together and securing them at the ankles.

"Now we will just wait for you to rejoin us and take care of business so he lasts longer for you," he said as he stood and pulled the chair around facing her; he sat a few feet from her. Exposing himself, he began masturbating and ejaculated almost immediately, staring at her beauty. She was deaf to his disgusting grunts and moans as he pleasured himself lusting over her.

CHAPTER 27

David was thankful that only one officer was wounded and one casualty from the other side was all that happened during the raids. They had managed to rescue twelve kids from the location he operated in and several others from the other locations. He hadn't heard the exact amount of the drugs seized, but he knew it was extensive and would certainly have an effect on those in the market.

The trauma and relief he saw on the faces of those kids made him want to go home and hug Gabriel even tighter. They had been turned over to protective services until they could be reunited with their families. They would have to answer several questions so they could try to identify any other suspects before being officially released.

David knew there was nothing further he could do since they had completed the task, and it was up to the government officials now, so he made his way back to where they had left their vehicles. He was grateful that the rain had begun to subside, making the hike back more tolerable. He allowed his thoughts to stray back to Aislinn and wondered why she hadn't answered any of his calls. He wondered if he had somehow frightened her off by coming on too strong, and he wrestled back and forth doubting himself.

"David, you need some sleep," he said out loud to himself, sighing relief when he caught sight of his Jeep ahead. He was able to see the sky getting a little lighter with probably another hour left until sunrise. He approached the Jeep and felt like he melted once he leaned back in the seat and reached in the console for his phone. He could see the flashing light indicating messages, so he looked at his missed call and saw that Aislinn had called. He pressed the voice mail button and listened to the voice tell him he had one message, so he leaned his head against the headrest and waited for the message to begin. Unable to hear some of the beginning, David restarted the message after turning the volume completely up on his phone. The message began again, and this time he was able to hear it more clearly. He could hear another voice, and it sounded like a male, but he couldn't make out clearly what was being said. He almost felt as if he were eavesdropping on a conversation for a moment until he could hear the tone in the man's voice.

David's heart nearly burst from his chest once he realized who the voice belonged to. He placed his phone on speaker and radioed out to the other officers. He checked the time of the call and discovered Aislinn had called nearly an hour earlier. He listened closely to the call and discovered the location where they crossed the county line. He requested to be patched through to the officers involved with setting up the roadblock in that vicinity and questioned if anyone had passed through resembling the description he provided. They advised they had seen a car with a woman driving who fit the description he had given. David immediately called out for backup and headed in the direction where they drove through. He was able to give more details as he continued listening to the rest of the message Aislinn had left.

Several officers were still in the area and caught up with David as he sped up the road at a high rate of speed, fearing he would be too late, since over an hour had elapsed since the call. He tried to time the call once they would have proceeded through the blockade to give him an indication of when he needed to slow down to look for tracks on the side of the road.

"Good girl," David said out loud as he spotted the ruts on the side of the road where she spun the wheels. He had heard the tires spin in the voice message, so he slowed his Jeep and turned on his high beams to follow the tracks that appeared to lead through an opening in the tree line of the woods. He followed them back nearly a mile when his headlights lit up a car that looked just like hers. He could see from his headlights that her car was vacant, so he pulled behind it and threw the Jeep in park. He remembered the direction they had taken also from the message on his phone and nearly ran up the side of the hill after grabbing his flashlight before the other officers even stepped from their cars. David followed the footprints left by Moran and Aislinn, and he was thankful the rain had stopped, preventing the tracks from being washed away completely.

David could hear the other two officers behind him, but they were still a few minutes away as he climbed along the roots of the tree leading upward. He hesitated briefly when he came to the edge and looked out over the ravine as dawn began to light the forest. It was still quite dark in the denser areas, so he still required the flashlight in the event he came to another drop just like the one he just passed. He stayed close to the edge as he followed the faint prints that followed around the large opening and was pleased to see the ground level out. He knew he was close from the smell of the smoke and nearly broke into a sprint following the sets of tracks. He broke through the drove of pines and killed his flashlight as he stared in wonder at the location of the cabin. He was going to have to stay low and use what remained of the dark to get close without being seen. The area was open and nestled back close to a rock mountainside, allowing the owners of the cabin total seclusion with the terrain hiding the cabin. He used the tree line to get closer to the cabin, hoping to get a glimpse through one of the windows. The glare on the panes forced him to get closer until he was directly under the window of the back door, crouched on the wood deck that went completely around the cabin on all sides. He could see the storage shed from his location several feet behind the cabin and noticed the tracks made from what appeared to be a dirt bike. He imagined that was where they kept their bikes and snowmobiles. He tilted his head to the side and peered in through the window. It was a direct view straight through the open design of the cabin and he could see Aislinn, who appeared to him to be unconscious and dangling from her wrists by a rope running over the big rafter.

He couldn't see Moran from this angle, so he crawled along the deck around to the front of the cabin to see if he could get a look through the picture window that showed the cascading view of the terrain running in front of the property. He could see Moran sitting in the chair with his back to the window, so David was able to see him from this angle with no fear of him seeing him first. He quickly spanned the remaining area to make sure no one else was there. This angle brought him a much clearer visual of Aislinn now, and he could see she was completely nude and in no position to defend herself from Moran. He could also tell Aislinn had been roughed up by someone and could only presume Moran was responsible.

David exited the porch when he saw the other officers approaching and wanted to provide them the assessment he had made of the situation. He was already disgusted by what he saw and hoped they arrived before Moran had the opportunity to do anything besides the physical abuse that was already evident. He met them briefly in the tree line and advised them of the situation. He wanted them to take the back since they wouldn't have a complete view of Aislinn's nudity and he could possibly cover her before they saw anything more than her breasts from their positions. It was apparent to him she had already been humiliated enough by Moran and his abusive treatment of her, and he wanted to spare her further embarrassment.

The three of them took their positions while the other two awaited David's signal to proceed with entry. He crouched by the window again, and he could see Aislinn begin to move her head about as she slowly regained consciousness. He was unable to see Moran's face because his back was to him, but he saw his posture change as he sat there in front of her, staring at her. He watched as she pulled at the restraint holding her arms over her head and tried to move her feet, but they were bound at the ankles. She raised her head and looked at Moran with a look of defiance, and for a moment, David thought she was looking directly at him through the window. He could see her mouth begin to move but was unable to hear the words she spoke to Moran.

David watched as Moran moved from the seat and walked directly in front of Aislinn where he stood for several seconds before reaching up and taking both of her breasts in his hands and bending to take one in his mouth while Aislinn pulled at the restraints. He couldn't watch anymore, and he wanted to stop Moran now before he made it further down as he made his way down her body with his tongue. David could see him knelt in front of her, pulling at the ropes that bound her ankles. Moran tossed the rope to the side and began spreading her legs farther apart as she fought against her other restraint. David's heart raced faster than he had ever remembered, and he could feel a rage come over him he had never experienced as he stood to make his way toward the front door. He knew that Moran's current position prevented the other officers from having a clear shot of him without the possibility of hitting Aislinn. For the first time in his life, he wanted to kill another human, and with that feeling came the recognition of his deeply profound love for Aislinn, so he took a step back to regroup.

CHAPTER 28

A islinn was beginning to have feeling in her legs again as the blood raced through her veins at the repulsion she felt at Moran touching her body. He had made his way down between her thighs and paused briefly from his onslaught of bites to her inner thighs to gaze at what appeared to be a scar in the shape of the letter *M* covered by a small tattoo of some female warrior directly above her shaved vaginal area.

"I am going to enjoy this," Moran jeered in a singsong manner. "I see I get to finish what I started, and trust me, I will finish it this time."

Aislinn twisted her body, trying to move away from him as she watched him remove his pants in front of her. He took his penis in his hand and pulled away briefly to show her his full size. Aislinn kicked at him with her legs, trying to get enough distance between them to use his body as leverage to help her get higher up his body and use the rope to her advantage if she could get her hands to work.

Moran laughed and pulled her close against him as he rubbed himself against her, becoming more excited the more she resisted. He brought his mouth down over hers roughly, and she opened her mouth to bite him, but he moved away quickly and laughed louder, warning her he loved a fight. He pulled her up roughly and positioned himself to enter her, and as he tried to force himself inside, she drew back her head and brought it forward, and with all of the force she had, she smashed her forehead into his nose, and as fell backward, she kicked him between the legs, causing him to drop to the floor and gasp.

The front door flew open, and she could see David coming through, but her eyes went back to Moran who had brought himself to a standing position and letting out a scream as he lunged toward her. She could see he had drawn a knife from his pants and had it held above him with a look of rage in his eyes and determination.

"I am going to cut your heart out, bitch!" he yelled, lunging in her direction with the knife extended above him. Moran seemed oblivious to David's presence and continued toward Aislinn with the knife extended and refused to drop it. David fired a shot, hitting Moran in the right shoulder, but he did not stop and lunged toward Aislinn with the knife, unfazed by his wound. Aislinn and David both watched as Moran fell to the floor inches in front of her from the bullet that penetrated the side of his head from one of the other officers. He quickly retrieved a throw from the armchair and wrapped it around her while the other officer cut the rope from her wrists. She fell against David, who had been holding her up, and allowed him to continue holding her for several minutes before taking the chair Moran had pulled over. Holding the blanket close to her, she listened as one of the officers requested medical assistance while the other stood over Moran, confirming he was dead after several minutes.

Aislinn could hear her name being called, but it was as if the voice were far off, and everything in front of her became a blur as she succumbed to the shock of what she had been through. She could feel David's arms around her, and she allowed herself to rest against his chest where he had moved her to the sofa in order for her to be closer to the fire.

David knew from the blank stare in her eyes it was useless to question her further about the incident and figured after she was able to receive the medical attention she required and much needed rest, she would be quite detailed in her explanation. He could only assume she had discovered information they prefer she hadn't or she asked the wrong question to the wrong person, leading them to believe she knew more than they wanted anyone to know. Either way, it nearly cost her life.

Aislinn lifted her arm to help David with putting her dry robe back around her and lay back on the couch once more as he draped the cover back over her for warmth. He placed a few logs on the fire because he knew it would be sometime before everyone would arrive and they would finish their investigation on the incident, but his main priority was keeping Aislinn comfortable until the medics arrived.

"They should arrive soon, sir," one of the officers informed him. "I am sorry we couldn't get a better shot earlier and that she had to endure that pig."

"I understand, Officer. You did what you needed to do, and at the end of the day, that's all anyone can expect," David assured him, not wanting him to take responsibility away from the perp.

"I couldn't take an earlier shot because it may have hit her," he continued to explain in a sense of embarrassment David could feel, as well as his own. He felt a tinge of guilt himself for not having been able to intervene prior to Moran assaulting her, but he was pleased he had fired the warning shot before shooting Moran to disable him when he had been so enraged moments before entering the cabin. He wanted to kill him but upheld his oath and the law although he knew it was a struggle to take any human life. No matter how bad others may believe some deserve it, he was still thankful he didn't have to take the head shot himself. He asked the officer if he needed to discuss it, and he said he was good for now, so David turned his attention back to Aislinn and watched her as she stared out the window from the sofa at the sunrise coming up through the trees and painting the sky a bright red and orange before quickly turning to yellow.

She laid her head back against the pillow, and he watched as her eyes slowly closed and the tenseness that covered her face began to relax, leaving the soft look he was used to seeing on her. He listened as she took a deep breath and fell into a deep sleep, unstirred by the whirring of the chopper landing in front of the cabin. He watched as they loaded her onto the gurney and transported her to the chopper, where he asked where they would be taking her. He was told they were given instructions to transport her to St. Mary's of Michigan in Saginaw, which would take David about an hour to drive once he reached the main road after beginning the hike back to his Jeep. They had given her a sedative before putting her in the chopper, so he figured he would make it in plenty of time before she would awaken. He made his way down the path after providing his statement of the events that occurred and called Mary as soon as he reached his vehicle to let her know he would be gone again.

"Hough here," David spoke into his phone, placing the call on speaker as he made his way to the hospital. He had learned from the caller that the cabin belonged to the officer killed by Moran and the others. He was also advised they had located several items believed to be the killers they were sending for analysis. "Did they notice any signs of anyone else in the area?"

He was met with a disappointing negative from the caller just before he ended the call. David was perplexed by Moran taking Aislinn to the cabin of the dead officer, and if it were in fact related to the death of that family, then why didn't the killer take advantage of Moran's presence and kill him like the others? he questioned, trying to make sense of the situation. Did the killer figure there would be trouble since Moran had abducted the reporter, possibly trying to frame them for that murder as well and bow out from having the pleasure of doing to him what they had done to the others, or had they met up with Moran and he was somehow able to do what the others had failed to? He would make a call and request they do a thorough search of the grounds and along any of the trails that look fresh to see if they could locate any remains that might potentially be the killer.

Kevin assured David he would request a thorough search for any remains and that the cabin had been searched both inside and out for anything that might provide them with answers. He told him they found a journal left by the officer in a hidden drawer of a chest in one of the bedrooms of the cabin, and it had details of events, as well as names of those involved. He said the journal also stated he was led to believe that he and his family were at risk of eminent harm because he believed the person he had reported the events to somehow managed to warn those involved, and they were intending to cause harm to him.

It stated they had been following him and undermining his work, making him appear to be unstable. He wrote that they had offered him a bribe to remain silent, but he stated he knew that even if he took it, they would manage to find a way to be rid of him. Kevin explained that everything the officer had recorded was factual information, and he felt it was necessary to reinvestigate the death of the officer and his family.

If everything he had recorded were in fact true, Kevin told David it would only be right that his honor be restored within the force and the community he served. Kevin explained they were able to get several of the others involved in the raids to give the names of those who ran the operation, and each of the murder victims' names came up as key players. He felt that everything was beginning to make sense, but he said it still doesn't give us the ID of the killer. They had performed checks into relations to the officer and his wife and found out he had been an only child and his wife had a sister, but she lived in Oregon and had been advised the entire family had been killed. They checked to see if there had been any recent travels by her, and it checked out that she had been at work and had not missed any days since her vacation last year.

David told Kevin he would check what had been created in the file by those involved in the cover-up and get back to him once he had a chance to have a look. He hung up the phone and finished the last few minutes of the drive to the hospital both exasperated and grateful. He couldn't believe they had been able to pull off such a crime without internal affairs being all over it, but it seemed these men had not only the town wrapped up but also a few higher-ups who, it appears, didn't follow protocol and possibly involved themselves.

David pulled in the emergency entrance parking lot and made his way into the lobby area; approaching the two ladies at the desk, he showed them his badge and asked to be escorted to Aislinn's room. One of the ladies informed him they had her in X-ray to make sure she didn't have any broken ribs or fractures to her face and skull, and they would take him back as soon as she returned. He took a seat facing the window and waited for them to call him.

CHAPTER 29

Aislinn awoke several hours later from the sedation and looked over to see David asleep in the chair next to her. She could tell that he had been there for sometime because his face was unshaven and his hair disheveled. He stirred when she moved to get comfortable in the bed and immediately he sat upright and smiled at her.

"Hi," he greeted, wiping his hands over his face and running them through his hair as he leaned forward to lift himself from the chair and stretch. "I'm sorry I dozed off."

"I don't think I would have noticed," Aislinn replied, aware that she had been asleep herself for several hours. "I could really go for a nice hot cup of coffee."

"Let me check with the nurse and see what I can do to make that happen," David assured her as he opened the door to her room and walked the short distance to the nurses' station. Minutes later, he returned with a piping hot Styrofoam cup full of the hot brew and handed her two containers of her favorite creamer.

"That is so thoughtful of you, and you remembered my creamer." Aislinn thanked him as she took a sip from the cup after adding the creamer.

"Some people are worth paying attention to." David smiled, taking the seat next to the bed and sipping the black brew from his own cup. "It's good to know that you will also be fine after enduring several X-rays and tests. They concluded you have bruising, abrasions, and a mild concussion, but otherwise doing well."

"Did they mention when they will release me?" Aislinn asked, hoping she could leave soon. She never liked hospitals or going to the doctor, and had she been coherent enough to make the decision, she would have chosen not to have gone and treated her abrasions herself. She expected to be sore for several days from the bruising, but it wasn't anything she wouldn't recover from.

"I believe they want you to speak with a counselor prior to being released by the physician, plus they want to keep an eye on the concussion." David assured it was for her own good as he had advised them she would be alone.

"So it is you who I have to blame for this?" she questioned with a smile crossing her face.

"I needed to make sure that you were well cared for," David said in a serious tone. "You really might want to consider a different field of journalism, one that is much safer than investigative. What if I hadn't made it there in time to protect you?"

"I have to say that coming from someone who works in a field where there is the potential to be shot daily, I am calling that a double standard," Aislinn argued, appearing insulted by his words. "A number of people take risks daily to perform their job duties. I don't believe that my choice is any different than yours, a doctor, or a social worker. Each of these options has benefits as well as risks."

"You have made a valid point, and I concur," David agreed, still seeming uncomfortable but not willing to express his reasons for being that way.

"David, I understand and appreciate your concern for my well-being, and I know that it is difficult for you to not be protective, but I can promise you that I have this," Aislinn tried to convince him.

"That's why Moran nearly killed you?" David argued back, unwilling to bend on his part.

"That didn't happen though, did it?" Aislinn asked, refusing to back down herself. "I realize I should have been more forthright with you and things may not have gotten so out of hand, but in the end, you were there and that is all that matters now."

"This time I was there, but who will be there the next time or the time after?" David asked, knowing she wouldn't bend either. "No story is worth risking your life."

"It is if it sets others free, David," Aislinn said softly. "You know as well as I that people like Moran would have managed to avoid spending any time and most likely would have had nothing more than a slap on the wrist as a first offender regardless of the number of lives he and the others impacted in a very negative way. The same rules don't apply for people like them because of their friends who will always protect them, but those same people will turn a helping hand away from anyone below their class status committing the same offense. It needs to be fair and equal for all, but it isn't, and that is shameful. I honestly don't blame the killer for seeking their own justice. They knew that the corruptness ran so deep in the political realm they would not see their vindication unless they acted themselves."

David understood and respected her words. Aislinn wouldn't be the person she is if she weren't able to help others who otherwise had no one in their corner fighting for them. She believed in following the truth, but their views differed in some aspects.

"Regardless of the crime committed, I think we often times forget that no matter what the person has done, they all have a mother, brother, sister, possibly even a child of their own who love them and need assurance their loved one is safe," David began his explanation of his view. "I am not their judge. I merely follow the laws, and if they break them, it is my duty to see that they are tried in a court of law regardless how corrupt some of the system has become. That is why we have checks and balances, but it seems some of the checkers fell asleep. My role will always be the peace officer because most of the time people just want to be validated in their feelings. I do my best to allow them their expression unless it impedes on others. Vigilante justice can get innocent people hurt."

"It doesn't appear to me that this particular killer hurt anyone that could qualify as innocent," Aislinn interjected, still defending the actions of the killer.

"Aislinn, it isn't that I disagree with what you are saying," David started again. "I just feel that if they had truly wished to follow the law, they would have contacted someone they could trust and allow them to investigate. You don't just go around slicing and dicing people up because they wronged you."

"Looking at the example these men set for the killer, I can understand why they would be hard-pressed to trust another law enforcement agent," Aislinn disagreed again, continuing her explanation. "Maybe the killer had seen the results of trying to follow the laws and discovered it got them nowhere, so they decided to dish out their own method of justice, which, according to what I have learned, was a dose of their own medicine. How could punishing someone with imprisonment for doing back what had been done to them be justice? It seems to me another method of oppression."

"I understand what you are saying too," David replied, running his hands through his hair as he chose his words wisely. "I have to ask one question though. If the killer is in fact acting on an event that took place over fifteen years ago, have they lived life throughout those years? I mean, think of it this way. They have relived whatever took place repeatedly for over fifteen years just to get to this moment of their plan. What has it gotten them, and where has any healing occurred?"

"Maybe this is what it took for them to heal, David," Aislinn responded to his questions. "We don't know what happened to this person or what was taken from them that would lead them to act out this type of vengeance. My guess would be it had to be pretty gruesome and some things you never get over, but you learn to put it away and allow other things to replace it. There are a lot of things that don't add up with the O'Conner family, and I have a suspicion that the little girl, Abigail, wasn't the child in the car that day. In fact, I have some information of who I think she is. I know this sounds crazy, but I think Abigail O'Conner is alive, and she came back to see that her family's name was cleared."

"I don't think you're crazy, Aislinn. In fact, there is some truth to what you said, but Abigail, I am not certain of," David stated, showing he had reasonable doubt. "Why would they kill an entire family and leave her alive only to stage her death with another little girl?"

"Maybe they thought she was dead, but she wasn't, and suddenly they needed to come up with a body to go along with the story they had fabricated for this horrendous act. What if she actually got away, David?" Aislinn explained, leaving him questioning the possibility.

"That would allow one to be nearly undetectable and not considered a suspect." David began to see what Aislinn was saying. He told her about the journal they found in the cabin, which gave them detailed events and names they could verify as evidence of truth. He questioned if the killer hadn't known Moran would go after Aislinn and had it set up so that she could be certain he would die, but she wouldn't want to miss the opportunity to watch it happen. David had a feeling there was no way she would take the opportunity to flee undetected without first making sure Moran was dead. He didn't believe she would watch him be taken in. His mind raced in different directions, but he did note that he referred to the killer as she now and had felt all along they displayed feminine movements, so he was encouraged that his intuition had not steered him incorrectly.

Aislinn lay against the pillow in bed and listened as David talked out loud the thoughts that ran through his mind. He had been creating a profile of the killer, and she was impressed with how close she felt he had come to her own idea of who she believed the killer to be. Her initial interest began with a top story with the impaled prosecutor, but her desire to stay was the handsome detective. It was fortunate for her she stuck around so that she could watch as the killer's justice unfolded right before her eyes. She admired David's pureness of heart and found that to be one of the qualities that had made her fall in love with him in the first place. She had been rooting for him all along, but she knew she could go places he would never get by with, so she did what she does best in her field and dropped as many clues as she could. She was impressed that little needed be told once she discovered how quickly he was able to find things on his own.

It was a shame to her what happened to his wife because she saw the pain he had to live for the poor choice of another person. David was always so forgiving, which seemed to make him shine more than most people she had met. She felt he was a top-of-the-line father who paid attention to the needs of his son and was hard-pressed to raise him to be a fine and honest young man. She adored this man and wanted to give him all of her, but she didn't feel that all of her was good enough for him. She saw the look in his eyes when he failed to take the head shot on Moran, who nearly stabbed her if it hadn't been for the other officer. She knew he realized in that instant he nearly cost her life, and she watched something slowly die in David she never wanted to see again although she could sense his relief at not having been the one who took the deadly shot.

"The problem is, how do you get others to see the potential when there was a body believed to be Abigail?" David asked, truly pondering her idea she could be alive. He had no doubt there were just as many people who would risk their lives to help another as there were those willing to take advantage. There were a number of possibilities and what-ifs, but he needed evidence, something tangible to prove the potential of her being alive.

"What if I was able to provide you with enough evidence to cause reasonable doubt that the child buried was Abigail?" she asked, as if she had been reading his mind. "We have already concluded that Moran and the others murdered the officer and his family because he discovered their crimes and couldn't be bought. Moran told me everything they did and where it all took place. He thought that I had somehow figured out their crime and was friends with Abigail and had been helping her. He told me that he shoved her from the ridge along the trail that Moran took me, so there has to be some truth to her existence."

"He gave you the location where they actually murdered the O'Conner family?" David asked in near disbelief. This would answer a lot of questions the townspeople pondered all these years but were too frightened to talk about. It was going to take a lot of healing in the community with everything that transpired then and recently, but he hoped to help lead it into a strong one. "I will send some men out to check the location and see if they can come up with anything since there have been so many years passed."

"That's not going to happen without me there," Aislinn stated in a matter-of-fact tone. "I plan to be there for the exclusive, David. After all, Moran revealed it to me. I want to be there to see it for myself."

David was surprised by Aislinn's sudden change in demeanor but dismissed it as nerves from her prior trauma. After reflecting on it briefly, he felt she was correct in requesting to be present since she was the only person at this time who knew the location. She had been respectful throughout the ordeal and assisted him with first-hand information without revealing it. He agreed that she deserved the exclusive and had nearly lost her own life obtaining it. She had been a key player in uncovering the activities of the recent murder victims, which, in turn, led to the recent raids, putting a dent in their operation.

"I'm sorry. You are absolutely right," David apologized, feeling he had been putting pressure on her regarding her career. She was very good at what she did, and he may not have gotten as far in the case as he had if it weren't for information she provided him. "But what if the killer gets away, Aislinn?"

"They already have, David," she calmly replied, rubbing her temples lightly from the mild headache she still had even with the pain medication they provided at the hospital. "The killer is gone."

"How can you be certain of that?" David asked, excited over the idea they may have already left.

"She left after Moran died," Aislinn replied one last time before lying back in the bed and allowing herself to succumb to the medication.

David was left to wonder if she had seen something they had missed or if the killer had given her information that would lead her to suspect they'd already left. It seemed he wasn't the only one being fed information by the killer, and he wondered why Aislinn had withheld it from him until now. He stood and walked to the nurses' station to tell them he would return once he had the opportunity to shower and take care of a few things, leaving them his number in case they needed to contact him.

On his way through town, he stopped by the office to pick up the O'Conner file and check his incoming mail before heading to his house to shower and do his best to look as if he'd joined the living again.

CHAPTER 30

Aislinn spent the remainder of the day and night in the hospital and was released the following morning. David had taken the liberty of buying her a T-shirt, sweats, and flip-flops for the drive back to Clare. They had called him earlier that morning and explained they would be releasing her at 9:00 a.m. after the doctor saw her. He could see that she had showered and pulled her hair back in a tight ponytail. Her movements were still slow from the bruising of her rib cages and mild vertigo from the concussion, but she seemed eager to leave. She slid the sweats on under the hospital gown, dropped the gown, and pulled the T-shirt over her head, uninhibited by his presence.

David was surprised by her lack of care and his inability to turn away as he stared at the curve of her breasts and her small waist. The reaction he had to the magnitude of her beauty hit him, and he excused himself, explaining he would wait for her in the hall.

Aislinn slid her feet into the flip-flops, grabbed the bag with her medications, and followed him into the hall where he and the attendant waited with the wheelchair to escort her from the hospital. She reluctantly climbed in after a disapproving look from David, and he led the way down the hall to the elevator. Aislinn's strong will was more prevalent, and she appeared to him to still be under the influence of the pain medication they prescribed her.

David imagined the drive back would prove to be interesting, but to his surprise, she sat quietly in the driver's seat, staring out the passenger window. He had, at one point, reached to turn the radio on and instead withdrew his hand, not wanting to disturb her thoughts she seemed so lost in.

"A penny for your thoughts," he whispered softly, but it appeared his words had gone unheard or that she had possibly fallen asleep. He was unable to see her face from the angle she was turned, and the sun reflecting from the window didn't cast her reflection in it. He realized she had gone through a tragic event and would need some time to recuperate. He couldn't help but wonder what she would do now that the story was coming to an end for her, but something inside him said she was leaving. He wanted her to stay with everything in him, but he wanted it to be her choice. He knew his life here was much different than her fast life and travels. He had fooled himself into thinking he could possibly keep her happy living in the woods with a ready-made family in a small town. He couldn't help but wonder if she had thought even for a moment about staying. He felt that he had made his feelings for her quite clear and had shared many personal things with her that he hadn't spoken with anyone else about.

Aislinn didn't want to face him because she was unable to control the tears that streamed down her cheeks and onto her lap. She hadn't intended to care for David, but trying to find a way to tell him goodbye was hurting her more than she had imagined she could ever hurt. He had found a way deep in her heart she never thought possible by anyone, but why was she surprised? she asked herself when she recognized why. It was the qualities he reflected that endeared him to her. She did her best to regain her composure and used the bottom of her shirt to wipe the tearstains from her face and turned in her seat to glance in his direction. She could see the strain on his face, and it stabbed at her heart, but she was able to keep herself together and told him the location of where Abigail's family had been murdered and where Abigail had been repeatedly assaulted, raped, and left for dead herself. He followed Aislinn inside where she described to David everything she knew that had been confessed to her by Moran and the killer.

David looked around the room and listened intently to Aislinn's story, which bore graphic details of what had taken place in the very place they stood. He was appalled by the torture the family had endured and couldn't believe that those responsible were the very ones who were there to protect and uphold the law. He questioned why no one in the community had shared their concerns with him, but he could understand their reservations when they were left to imagine what happened to the one man who stood up for the law ends up dead along with his family. David had no doubt that most had a healthy fear of what knowing too much could cost them, so they buried their heads in the sand to protect their own families. Trusting that you could talk openly with anyone affiliated with law or the courts might not be in one's best interest when the examples they had weren't good.

Several minutes passed and Aislinn hadn't said anything further, so David touched her arm and suggested they go back outside where they can breathe the air and he could make a couple of calls. She followed him back into the sunshine and held her face toward it, and she could feel the warmth of its rays on her face as she listened to David provide the details to the person on the other end so they could dispatch a team to the site and possibly confirm everything Aislinn had been told. The same team who assessed the cabin showed up within thirty minutes of the call with their gear, ready to test the area for signs of old blood since it sounded like there would have been a lot. David was impressed with all the new technology used today relevant in determining facts in old cases.

They drove in town for a cup of coffee and picked a corner booth where they sat sipping at their cups of steaming brew, going over their discoveries while they waited for any results to come back from the team.

Aislinn stressed how she was relieved that the truth about the O'Conner family would be revealed and Officer O'Conner's name would be cleared. She told David it was bad enough the man was murdered for doing the right thing and then to have them taint his reputation the way they had should merit an honorary plaque in his name or a memorial for his entire family.

David agreed that if they could determine this were the true facts, he and his family should be honored and remembered, but that still left the question as to whether or not Abigail had been a victim or was still alive.

"Where is she, Aislinn?" David asked, reaching across the table and covering her free hand with his, hopeful she had the information and would share it with him.

"I don't know where she is, David, but I do know she's gone," Aislinn replied, lifting her hand and caressing the side of his face, knowing after he dropped her off it would be the last time she would ever see him, so she took in everything she could about him—his smile, his laugh, the way he moves his mouth when he speaks, how he uses his hands to emphasize his words, and the light that seemed to always be present in his eyes. The memories would have to be enough she told herself as she prepared to let go, watching him as the information began coming through. She already knew the results and wasn't surprised when he shared with her what they had uncovered.

Aislinn kept herself together as David drove her to the cottage and explained that her car had been thoroughly checked and cleaned as she seemed surprised to see it sitting where she usually parked it. He stepped from the Jeep and opened the driver's side door and reached beneath the seat of her car before approaching the passenger door to help her step down. He waited for her to have her balance before proceeding down the path, holding her arm in his for stability, and paused in front of her when they reached the door. Without a word or hesitation, she leaned upward to kiss him. She placed her hands behind his head and pulled him down to her as she kissed him deeply.

David pulled her to him but was careful not to put too much pressure on her ribs as he returned the kiss. She pulled at him as her desire for him climbed higher and higher. She craved his touch; with each stroke of his hand on her body, she could feel the nerve endings screaming out for more. She fumbled with the keys in the lock and nearly dropped them as his mouth trailed kisses down her neck until he reached the nape where he sucked gently at first, causing her to lose herself in the feelings that now overwhelmed her. She was consumed by the fire that burned deep within her, and the feeling of his hardness pressing against her lower abdomen was one she wondered if she would ever feel. She had never experienced these feelings with any man and wondered if she could ever live without them again.

She closed the door behind them, and before David could say anything as it appeared he was trying to find the words, she untied the string to her sweats and allowed them to fall to the floor before pulling the T-shirt over her head and releasing her hair from the band that secured it, allowing her hair to fall down her back. She dropped the T-shirt to the floor next to her and stepped easily from the bottoms as she made her way in front of him again. David dropped to his knees and placed his head against her stomach, gently stroking her back and running his fingers softly over her ribs. He began to softly kiss her midriff, slowly working his way to her breasts and back down, until she thought she would explode from deep inside her. She pulled at his shirt until he released her long enough to slide it over his head; pulling her against him again, the feel of his skin against hers sent sparks igniting throughout her body.

The pleasure he created in her caused her to cry out in ecstasy as she felt her body writhing against his in anticipation of feeling him completely. David slowly worked his way down, allowing his mouth to linger over the tattoo that surprised him when he first saw it. He found it attractive and fitting for her, and the way she responded when he ran his tongue over it drove him to want to please her more. He dipped his tongue inside her, and the soft moans grew louder until he was drowning in the sound of her as her body rose and fell with each spasm. Her skin was covered in a light mist as he stood to remove his pants. Her eyes were heavy and dreamy as he gazed in them while she stared at him, anxious for his touch.

Aislinn was concerned that she wouldn't be able to satisfy him, but it seemed that everything came natural to her regarding him. They spent several hours learning each other and enjoying the response as they caressed and kissed and made love several times throughout the night.

David had to leave early so that he could see Gabriel off to school and stop by the office to see if the information he awaited had come, but he promised her he would return as quickly as he could before reluctantly throwing on his clothes after holding her and kissing her several more times.

Aislinn kissed him and handed him the key to her cottage so that he could let himself back in, knowing she wouldn't be there when he returned. If she didn't leave now, she would likely never leave. She watched as he walked up the path to his Jeep and waved as he pulled away. She closed the door and began composing a letter, explaining why she needed to leave, hoping he would understand her unselfish reasons behind doing so. She was very clear in expressing her feelings for him so that he would not be mistaken in believing there was nothing between them.

She picked the paper up and placed it to her lips where she kissed it gently before laying it to the side and began packing her belongings, leaving out a casual outfit for the drive. She showered quickly and threw her hair in a ponytail, not wanting to spend any time on it. She dressed and began loading her car, uncertain where she planned to go, but she knew she would figure that out once she set out. She was certain she needed to leave now, though, because if he returned or she passed him driving, she would never be able to walk away. He was the one person she would absolutely lay her life down for.

CHAPTER 31

O Captain! My Captain! Our
Fearful trip is done,
The ship has weather'd every
Rack, the prize we sought is won,
The port is near, the bells I
hear, the people all exulting.
While follow eyes the steady
Keel, the vessel grim and
daring;
But O heart! heart! heart!
O the bleeding drops of red,
Where on the deck
Captain lies,
Fallen cold and dead.

O Captain! my Captain! rise
Up and hear the bells;
Rise up-for you the flag is
flung-for you the bugle trills,
For you bouquets and
ribbon'd wreaths-for you the
shores
a-crowding.
For you they call, the swaying
mass, their eager faces
turning;
Here Captain! dear father!

This arm beneath your head!
It is some dream that on the
Deck,
You've fallen cold and dead.

My Captain does not answer,
His lips are pale and still,
My father does not feel my
Arm, he has no pulse nor Will,
The ship is anchor'd safe and
Sound, its voyage closed and
Done,
From fearful trip the victor
ship comes in with object
won;
Exult O shores, and ring O
bells!
But I with mournful tread,
Walk the deck my Captain
lies,
Fallen cold and dead.

—Walt Whitman, *Leaves of Grass*

The stranger left the book lying open to the page and gathered her few belongings, placing each of them carefully into her back-pack—photos, her mother's favorite necklace, her brother's favorite stuffed animal, and a couple of children's books her parents read to her frequently in her younger years—and placed them in the back seat of her car. She started the car, but before proceeding, she scribbled a note to drop in the mail to the detective which read, "You are a man of honor and integrity, Detective. It's refreshing to discover those qualities still exist and the uniform is being properly repre-sented. I understand your belief that I have committed crimes of murder, but I ask you, how does a ghost commit murder? They mur-dered me the day they came after my family. The person I was could never be again, so I became someone else. You see, had they changed their ways or even possibly shown some remorse for what they did, I may have forgiven them. They chose to continue to harm others, so I chose their punishment based on what they did not only to me but also to the many others who are unable to fight for themselves. I don't need a system to substantiate or validate what they did to me, for I know and yet I remain remarkably unbroken. The only thing broken is a judicial system with no justice."

She dropped the letter off in the mailbox nearest the end of town and edged the gas pedal harder as she felt the gear kick in as it gained speed. She adjusted herself in the seat and watched the city of Clare disappear through her rearview mirror. She would do what she could to find some semblance of life since everything pertaining to her life had led up to this moment in time, and now it was over and she hadn't considered what she would do after. She pontificated whether or not she had possibly planned on not making it out alive, but she had, and now she would have to resolve what her next choices would be. After all, she could be anyone she wished to be.

CHAPTER 32

David enjoyed having breakfast with Gabriel before dropping him off at the school and driving to the office. He laughed at himself as he caught himself whistling on several occasions this morning and couldn't wait to return to Aislinn. He was confident she would be sleeping, and he wanted to give her more time to rest after he was sure he had drained her energy last night. He was feeling the effects of having been up all night, but he was very chipper and alert.

He greeted Pam and the others as he strolled down the hall to his office. He had several things he was hoping to have the answers to, and it appeared a few of them had come in. He perused through the papers that had been faxed to him and the mail stack set there by Pam before opening his e-mail and discovering Kevin had sent some important documents that the results came back from.

David was pleased by most of what he had read in the discoveries as he briefed his way through the information. It appeared it was as he had come to believe. Abigail's body had been replaced with a young lady whose parents had reported missing and had made reports that the photos of the family killed that had been made public resembled their daughter. They were told it was a coincidence. He was pleased they would be able to clear the officer's name who had been murdered and that of his family. David looked at the photo maturation that had been completed on Abigail, and he nearly fell out of his seat upon first glance. So many of the features resembled Aislinn, but it had to be coincidence, he thought. It was true that Abigail had been a very attractive child, and he could see where they might resemble one another since both were beautiful. There was nothing about Aislinn that remotely resembled the characteristics of a killer according to what he had been taught and everything he had learned obtaining his degree. There were moments he might have questioned who she was, but killer had never been one of them. Besides, he thought, she had been with him when a couple of the murders took place.

Putting it aside as mere coincidence, David laid the papers back in the file and hummed a tune on the way out of the office, anxious to see the one woman who had ever intrigued him beyond imagination.

He hadn't noticed her car was gone when he pulled in front of the cottage and made his way down the path. He was still floating on a cloud from that night and couldn't wait to be with her again. He hadn't been able to stop thinking about her from the first time they met at the coffee shop. Everything about her exceeded his imagination, and he had come up with what he felt was a perfect solution that would allow them opportunities to spend time together and both continue their careers, if she was still interested in pursuing what he considered the beginning of an amazing relationship.

David walked straight to the bedroom, and when he couldn't find her anywhere in the house, he noticed the hand-scribed note lying on the pillow of the bed. He clutched the note that expressed her feelings for him against his chest and read the last lines out loud.

"I cannot be awake for nothing looks to me as it did before, or else I am awake for the first time, and all before has been a mean sleep" (Walt Whitman).

About the Author

Laura was born and raised in a small town in southern Ohio. She attended Ohio University where she graduated cum laude while raising her three children. She was an adoption specialist for the state of Ohio and worked successfully with numerous underprivileged children and families toward achieving permanency for the children.

Laura has always had a passion for writing and provided research materials to author Dan Brown for his works *Angels and Demons* and *Deception Point*.

She enjoys traveling and has visited most of the United States and many countries of the world. She enjoys experiencing other cultures and has cultivated lasting friendships all over the world.

In addition to writing, Laura's greatest interests are her family, friends, art, and nature. She currently resides in a small rural Tennessee town.